You're just playi

Despite everything, T
responding to Hannah. Responding to the
intoxicating, sweet taste of her skin against his lips.

Dammit, get a grip, Colton.

Satisfied that he had performed as expected for
whatever camera or cameras hidden in the room,
Tate whispered the same message into Hannah's
ear that he'd told her yesterday.

"I'm here to rescue you," he told her.

He couldn't allow his guard to go down, not even
for a moment. "You and the others," he added.
"But this isn't going to be easy and I'm going to
need your help to pull it off."

Hannah turned her head slowly to look at him. He
could tell by the look in her eyes that he'd made a
breakthrough.

She was finally beginning to believe him.

Dear Reader,

We have exciting news for you! Starting in January, Harlequin Romantic Suspense is unveiling a brand-new look that's a fresh take on our beautiful covers. Turn to the back of the book for a sneak peek.

There's more! Along with new covers, the stories will be longer—more action, more excitement, more romance. Follow your beloved characters on their passion-filled adventures. Be sure to look for the newly packaged and longer Harlequin Romantic Suspense stories wherever you buy books.

In the meantime, you can check out this month's adrenaline-charged reads:

CHRISTMAS CONFIDENTIAL by Marilyn Pappano and Linda Conrad

COLTON SHOWDOWN by Marie Ferrarella

O'HALLORAN'S LADY by Fiona Brand

NO ESCAPE by Meredith Fletcher

Happy reading!

Patience Bloom

Senior Editor

MARIE FERRARELLA

Colton Showdown

HARLEQUIN®
entertain, enrich, inspire™

Special thanks and acknowledgment to Marie Ferrarella for her contribution to The Coltons of Eden Falls miniseries.

Recycling programs
for this product may
not exist in your area.

ISBN-13: 978-0-373-27802-2

COLTON SHOWDOWN

Copyright © 2012 by Harlequin Books S.A.

Books by Marie Ferrarella

MARIE FERRARELLA

This *USA TODAY* bestselling and RITA® Award-winning author has written more than two hundred books for Harlequin Books and Silhouette Books, some under the name Marie Nicole. Her romances are beloved by fans worldwide. Visit her website, www.marieferrarella.com.

To
Sebastian Burgess,
Welcome to the world,
little guy

Prologue

Her face haunted him.

Ever since he'd seen her on that DVD, the one that had been made to showcase the "selection" available for purchase by the members of the "discerning" male audience viewing it, Detective Tate Colton had been equally fascinated and sick to his stomach.

Fascinated because Hannah Troyer, one of several young women displayed on the video, was at once hypnotically beautiful and so obviously innocent. And sick to his stomach because he knew what was going to happen to Hannah. Knew what was going to happen to *all* the innocent young women who appeared on the video. Each and every one of them was destined to become the object of some depraved pervert's lechery—as long as the right price was quoted and met.

Unless he and the FBI agents on his team got to those girls first.

Someone was kidnapping Amish girls and selling them to the highest bidder because in this jaded age of too much too soon, the idea of an untouched, pure young woman still held an almost addictive allure for some men.

In this case, the "some" were exceptionally wealthy men because innocence had become a commodity that did not come cheap. Instead, it was bade and bargained for like the rare product it had become, only to be forever lost at the hands of depraved men who had no idea how to rightly value such a treasure.

Eyes on the screen, Tate went back over the DVD and played it forward again, watching the same small section he'd viewed before of the girl he'd seen while going undercover as a prospective buyer.

Watching her.

Gray-blue eyes, alabaster skin, hair like flame.

They called her Jade. But she was Hannah Troyer.

He knew her name—her *real* name, only because Hannah's brother, Caleb, was desperately searching for his younger sister. The search had created strange bedfellows because, just recently, Caleb had wound up becoming engaged to his sister, Emma, a Special Agent with the FBI. They were working together on a joint task force to find the missing girls. According to what his sister had said, she and Caleb were going to be married once this case was finally wrapped up.

That made it sound so easy, Tate thought cynically. A piece of cake—and it wasn't.

There wasn't anything at all easy about this case. Not for the two dead girls they'd already found. Not for the whole of the small Pennsylvania Amish community— ironically called Paradise Ridge—which was holding its collective breath, waiting and praying for their own to be returned to them unharmed.

Tate had an uneasy feeling that wasn't possible. Even if they found all the other missing girls and they were still alive, they were no longer unharmed. Far greater than the physical scars they might have incurred were the emotional scars that had to run across their young, tender souls.

In this sex trafficking ring, the mostly faceless bastards who were abducting the young women were systematically destroying their innocence so that the girls—all between the ages of 16 and 20—bore little to no resemblance to the sweet young women their families were frantically searching for.

"I'd like to gut each and every one of those bastards," he muttered under his breath, finally shutting off the DVD player. The large screen he'd been watching went blank.

Emma, the only other person in the room with him, laughed shortly. There was no mirth in the sound. "You're not the only one who feels that way."

As she spoke, she put her hand on Tate's broad shoulder and was surprised by how rigid it felt. Well, maybe not so surprised, she silently amended. Tate, who'd been the one to initially ask her to join his task force, took his work very seriously, but this had to be a new level of intensity, even for him.

"I think that if we ever find the people who kidnapped Hannah, Caleb would be tempted to temporarily renounce his pacifistic ways, just for the time it would take to pummel these worthless scum into the ground. But indulging in fantasies isn't going to help us rescue these girls," Emma pointed out. "And we *are* going to rescue them," she told Tate with utter conviction, not for the first time.

Failure, as the saying went, was not an option here. There were too many lives at stake, too many families waiting to get their daughters back.

Tate knew he would have felt a personal obligation to bring the girls all back to their families even if the people affected by this heinous ring were *not* technically his neighbors.

The Colton family ranch in Eden Falls, Pennsylvania, was named the Double C in honor of Charlotte Colton. Charlotte was the woman who, even though she hadn't given them biological life, had, for all intents and purposes, along with her husband, Donovan, given him and his five siblings a reason to exist, a reason to live.

The couple, whose lives were so tragically cut short along with those of so many others on 9/11, were well-known for their dedication and their generosity. Over the course of two decades, they had adopted six completely unrelated orphans, given them their name and their love and knitted them into a family. A family who never took what they had for granted. The ranch where they grew up was right outside a little village named Paradise Ridge.

Civilization, with all its technological progress, seemed to have stopped at the borders of the tiny town. The hardworking citizens of that town led what was considered an idyllic life that echoed their ancestors' existence. Until a serpent somehow found its way into Paradise Ridge and stole some of the town's young women.

Tate was determined to find those girls and the ones from Ohio.

Especially, he silently promised the face that haunted

him, Hannah. Find them and free them. Even if it was the last thing he ever did on this earth.

"C'mon, Big Brother," Emma was urging him. "You and I have a sting to plan and coordinate."

Snapping out of his mental fog, Tate rose from the chair he'd taken to view the DVD for the umpteenth time, searching for some telltale clue he might have missed before.

He looked at his sister as they got ready to meet the others involved in this undercover operation. "Tell the truth, Tomato-head, you're going to miss this once you turn in your badge for a butter churn." He still loved to use her childhood nickname, to her annoyance.

Try as he might, he just couldn't picture his driven sister in that kind of laid-back, rural setting—not for more than ten minutes.

"No, I'm not," Emma countered with feeling. Then, when Tate's eyes held hers, she shrugged. "Well, maybe just a little," she allowed as they left the office. Because he'd forced the truth out of her, Emma punched his arm.

Tate's deep laugh echoed up and down the hallway. Maybe Emma wasn't going to miss this life, but he sure as hell was going to miss Emma.

Chapter 1

He wasn't one of those people who had an obsession about cleanliness. Tate Colton had never had a problem with getting his hands—or any other part of him, for that matter—dirty, if the job required it. That kind of dirt he could put up with and ignore.

But dealing with these subhuman creatures who made their living trafficking in human flesh, in destroying young lives and thinking absolutely nothing of it, was an entirely different matter. It made him want to go back to the hotel room where he was registered under his assumed name and take a shower. A long, scalding-hot shower to wash away their stink.

Once he received the assignment from his supervisor, Hugo Villanueva, he knew that going undercover in order to find and save the Amish young women who had been kidnapped would require him to associate with, in his opinion, the absolute dregs of the earth.

Dregs in expensive suits.

You could dress a monkey up in fine clothes, but he was still a monkey, Tate thought. No amount of expensive clothing could change that, or change the fact that the people he was forced to interact with were lower than scum.

He'd think more about stepping on a beetle than he would about terminating the existence of one of these cockroaches.

To look at the man who had brought him up to this particular hotel suite—his current tour guide to this underworld—someone might have thought the man was a successful businessman or the CEO of a Fortune 500 company instead of the utterly soulless lowlife that he actually was.

Impeccably dressed in what was easily a thousand-dollar suit, his guide to this lurid world of virgins-for-sale smirked at him confidently as he opened the door leading into the suite's bedroom.

"I'm sure we can find something to pique your appetite, Mr. Conrad," he said.

Tate scowled at the shorter man. "I said no names," he snapped, mindful of the part he was playing in this surreal drama.

The other man laughed, enjoying what he considered to be the display of ignorance on the part of this new client.

"Nothing to be worried about. What are they going to do?" he asked, gesturing at the bedroom and the young women being held there. Each and every one of them were dressed in identical long, slinky white gowns. "Post it on the internet? None of them even know what the hell the internet *is,*" he stressed, jeering at the young women who were virtually prisoners in this suite. "They all live in the Stone Age. Trust me." He patted Tate's arm and the latter shrugged him off as if he was flinging off an annoying bug—an act that wasn't lost on the man. "Your name—and your sterling reputation—are both safe here," he assured Tate.

"C'mon, c'mon," the man snapped at the young woman he was herding into the room for his "client's" final review. "He hasn't got all night. Or have you?" he asked, looking over his shoulder at Tate, a lecherous grin spread across his angular face. "You know, if you've changed your mind and want to make your purchase now—" He left the sentence open, looking at Tate expectantly.

"I haven't changed my mind," Tate answered formally. The deal was that he got to see the young women in person in order for him to finalize his choice, and then the negotiations regarding the pending "purchase" would go from there.

Inside, Tate was struggling to contain his fury. The woman he'd "requested," "Jade," was looking at him apprehensively like a mistreated animal afraid of being beaten.

Had she been beaten?

Tate looked her over quickly. "What's wrong with her?" he demanded, channeling his anger into the part he was playing—a man who wanted the "goods" he was considering purchasing to be perfect. He was well aware of the fact that the blue-gray eyes continued to watch his every move. Tate swung around to confront the other man. "She looks like she's been manhandled," he accused angrily.

The man shrugged indifferently. "Don't worry. Nothing happened that would have left a visible mark on her." His flat, brown eyes raked over Hannah from head to toe, as if to reassure himself that she wasn't displaying any sign of bruising in plain sight. "That's the one rule—other than payment up front—the boss won't tolerate any visible marks left on the merchandise."

Out of the corner of his eye, Tate saw Hannah flinch at the label the man had contemptuously slapped on her. *Merchandise*.

His anger flared.

"She's a person, not merchandise," Tate retorted, glaring at the guard.

"Hey, at the price you're going to pay, she's anything you want her to be. You want a person? You got it, she's a person." He turned to look at the redhead he'd led out of the bedroom for Ted Conrad's perusal. "A soft, sweet-smelling person, aren't you, honey?"

Smirking, he slid his hand along her cheek and down the side of her neck.

It was obvious that the guard didn't intend on stopping there.

"I'll thank you to take your hands off her," Tate warned darkly as the man's hand just grazed the swell of her breasts.

Anger flashed in the other man's eyes, but just as quickly, it subsided. The main reason he'd been told to bring this client here was to get Conrad to make his final decision so that the deal could proceed.

Apparently, it looked as if the deal was about to be sealed. The bottom line was, and had always been, money. So, much as he would have personally rather shot out this client's kneecaps, the guard raised his hands in the air in mock surrender.

"They're off," he declared dramatically, wiggling his fingers in the air to underscore his point. The smirk on his face deepened as he looked at Hannah knowingly. "So, this is the one you want, eh?"

"She's the one," Tate replied, his tone scrubbed free of any emotion.

The other man nodded his approval. "Gotta say, you've got good taste. She's a beauty." With hooded eyes, he looked her over again. It was obvious that he was putting himself in the client's place. "She also looks like she might last you awhile."

Hannah drew in a breath. They'd given them all some sort of pills, but she had managed to fool her captors into thinking she'd swallowed hers when she hadn't. Each word from the guard felt like a dagger, stabbing into her heart.

Her eyes swept over both men. "Please don't do this," Hannah pleaded.

It was impossible to know which of them she addressed her plea to.

For his part, though he took care not to show it, Tate felt terrible. He could certainly imagine what was going through Hannah's mind. What Caleb's sister was anticipating. He would have given anything to comfort her, but that wasn't what was going to save her.

In order to accomplish that, he had to be convincing in his role. Which meant that he needed to go on with this charade, continue to maintain this facade so that he could, ultimately, get her and her friends away from these men.

If he went about it the traditional way, pulling out a service weapon and threatening to shoot the other man if he got in his way, Tate knew that he might—or might not—be able to get out of the hotel with Hannah. Most likely, they'd be stopped before they ever made it to the street level.

No, this way was more effective. It just required a great deal of focus and an iron will—and the ability to block out that look in her eyes to keep it from getting to him.

"What did I tell you about opening your mouth?" the guard was demanding angrily. He pulled back his hand, ready to bring it down on her face.

Hannah's alarmed cry tore at his heart.

"If she has one mark on her, the deal's off," Tate warned him in a voice that was deadly calm, belying the turmoil that lay just beneath.

The guard stopped in midswing. The expression on his face told Tate that the guard was getting fed up with what he undoubtedly considered a high-and-mighty client. The man let his guard down for a second, the sneer on his face telling Tate that he thought he knew his type. Not just knew it, but hated it because he felt inferior to the supposedly rich client.

"You don't buy her, someone else will," the guard jeered contemptuously. But he dropped his hand to his side nonetheless. "Sit!" he ordered Hannah with less compassion than he would have directed to a pet dog. Only when she complied did the guard finally look his way. "So, I take it we've got a deal. You're interested in acquiring this tasty morsel?"

Tate's expression gave nothing away, including the fact that he could easily vivisect him without so much as a thought. "I might be," he replied after a beat had gone by.

"Might be," the man echoed with contempt. He was at the end of his patience. "Look, the man I represent doesn't like having his time wasted. We're alike that way because neither do I."

Tate slowly walked around the young woman, deliberately pausing and taking a lock of her hair between his fingers. He made a show of sniffing it. "That goes both ways."

Suspicion immediately entered the guard's eyes. "So what do you have in mind?"

There was no hesitation on Tate's part. "A man doesn't buy an expensive car without taking it on a test run, seeing how it handles," he pointed out, his voice continuing to be flat.

It killed him to see that Hannah had winced again in response to his words, and he saw real fear in her eyes as she watched him.

How did he get it across to her that he was one of the good guys without blowing his cover?

"Go on, I'm listening," the other man said.

"I'd like a private session with her, to see how we 'get along,'" Tate proposed.

"The boss doesn't deal in damaged goods," the other man snapped.

"I have no intentions of 'damaging' her. Just 'sampling' her," Tate informed him. "There are a lot of ways a man can see if he likes the goods he's getting."

He was standing in front of Hannah now, looking into her eyes, wishing there was some way to set her mind at ease. His back was to the other man and he smiled at Hannah. The smile was kind, devoid of the lust that had supposedly brought him here. Lowering his head so that his lips were right next to the young woman's ear, he whispered, "Caleb sent me," before straightening and backing off.

Her eyes widened, but she held her tongue.

Tate said a quick, silent prayer of thanksgiving to whoever it was that watched over law enforcement officers.

"What did you say to her?" the guard demanded. There was no arguing with his tone.

Tate turned to look at him, emulating the latter's previous smug look. "I told her that paradise was at hand."

As he said that, Tate slanted a look toward Hannah, hoping she would put two and two together and take some comfort in the covert message. He couldn't tell by her expression if she'd believed him—or even understood what he was trying to tell her. He wasn't even sure if she'd heard him say that Caleb had sent him.

Terror, he knew, had a way of blocking out everything else.

The man relaxed a little, then laughed. "Good one," he pronounced. "That's where she and some of those other girls come from, some backward hole-in-the-wall called Paradise Ridge."

Tate tried to sound casually uninterested. A man making small talk, involved in a meaningless conversation that would be forgotten before he walked out the door. "Is that where all the girls are from? This Paradise Ridge place you just mentioned?"

His question was met with a nod. "This batch is. They picked up others from—" He abruptly stopped his narrative. His eyebrows narrowed over small, deep-set eyes. "What's with all the questions?"

Tate shrugged. "Just trying to find out how big a selection you've got—in case things don't work out with this one," he explained.

"Oh, it'll work out," the man promised. There was no room for argument. He looked at Hannah pointedly. "She knows what'll happen to her if it doesn't. Don't you, honey?" The smile on his lips was cold enough to freeze a bucket of water in the middle of May.

This time, instead of fear rising in Hannah's eyes,

Tate thought he saw anger. Anger and frustration because, he guessed, there was nothing she could do right now about the anger she was feeling.

The other man was apparently oblivious to her reaction. It was clear that fear was all he looked for, all he valued.

"Don't want to wind up like your girlfriends now, do you?" he taunted her.

Things suddenly fell into place. The annoying little troll was referring to the two dead girls Emma and Hannah's brother had initially discovered. Solomon Miller, a so-called "repentant" Amish outcast had brought them straight to the bodies, hoping to use the fact that he was informing on his "boss" as a bargaining chip.

Initially part of the group of men involved in the sex trafficking ring, Miller had become the task force's inside man, trading information for the promise of immunity once all the pieces of this case came together and they got enough on the men running this thing to take them to court—and put them away for the next century or so.

If they didn't wait until they discovered exactly who was behind all this and bring him—or her—in, if they just grabbed up the two-bit players they were dealing with in this little drama, the operation would just fold up and relocate someplace else.

And Amish girls would continue disappearing as long as there were sick men to make their abductions a profitable business.

No, they had to catch the mastermind in order for this operation to be deemed a success.

"Don't threaten her," Tate warned. When the guard shot him a malevolent look, he told him, "I want her to be willing to be with me, not because she was threatened with harm if she wasn't."

The guard looked at him as if he wasn't dealing with a full deck. "Hey, man, don't you know? It's better when they fight you."

The world would be a much better place if he could just squash this cockroach, Tate thought, struggling to hang on to his temper. With no qualms whatsoever, Tate would have been more than willing to put everyone out of their collective misery—himself included.

But instead, he was forced to tamp down his temper and nonchalantly tell him that "We each have our preferences."

"Yeah, well, you're the man with the bankroll," the guard grumbled resentfully.

"Yes, I am."

Tate was grateful for the elaborate lengths the department had gone to in order to give him a plausible backstory. His brother, Gunnar, had funded his huge bank account.

Whoever was running this sex trafficking operation wasn't a fool, Tate concluded. He was very, very careful to get everything right. That included vetting his clients rather than just accepting them at face value, or going with hearsay.

Nothing was simple anymore, Tate thought. Not even the peddling of flesh.

"So it's settled?" Tate asked the man. The blank look he received in return forced him to elaborate. "I can have a private session with her?"

"Soon as I run it by the boss" came the reply.

"And how long is that going to take?"

He knew things had to progress at their own pace, but he hated the idea of leaving the girl alone with this thug for another moment, much less for another day or two. There was no telling what could happen in that amount of time, and he didn't want to take any more chances than he had to.

"Anxious?" the other man jeered, enjoying himself. He liked having the upper hand and, in this case, he clearly got to call the shots. "Tomorrow. Come back tomorrow. She'll be ready for you then."

Just what did that scum mean by "ready"?

A premonition had a shiver zipping down Tate's back, but there was absolutely nothing he could do about the circumstances. Tate was well aware that if he pressed, if he remotely said that she looked ready now or tried in any way to hurry this along, the whole thing could just fall apart on him. There were steps to take and he knew it.

That didn't make taking them any easier.

If this was rushed, the people they were after would smell a setup and not just back off but vanish into thin air, taking the young women with them. He'd seen it before.

Hell, he'd *been* part of it before—having an operation unravel on him that allowed a killer to be set free. The man was ultimately taken down and brought to justice, but not before he'd killed several more young women. Young women who wouldn't have died if he had done his job right in the first place, Tate thought ruefully.

That wasn't going to happen again, he vowed. This time, he was going to do things by the book. Even if that meant he had to find a way to physically restrain himself.

"What time tomorrow?" he asked the guard.

"We'll get back to you about that," the man told him, affecting a superior attitude.

Tate narrowed his eyes, looking as cold as the man he was dealing with. Colder. "I don't like being jerked around," he said in a voice that contained an unspoken warning.

"Nobody's jerking you around," the other man promised, sounding more than a little nervous that this encounter could turn physical. "I'll call you tomorrow," he said again, this time far more amiably.

"I'll look forward to it," Tate said, not bothering to tone down the note of sarcasm in his voice. He looked from Hannah to the man, wondering if she even realized how breathtakingly beautiful she was. She reminded him of a rose newly in bloom. "In the meantime, I don't want anyone touching her."

The other man began to smirk again. "She really got to you, eh?"

Tate was aware that men like the one he was dealing with directly understood only one thing: money. It was the only language they spoke. However, he hadn't been given the suitcase that was to be filled with the cash he was to trade for Hannah. That came tomorrow.

Whatever cash he had on him at the moment was his own, but it was only paper as far as Tate was concerned. Paper that was capable of buying both him and Hannah a little peace of mind.

Taking out his wallet, Tate removed a hundred-dollar bill. As the other man eagerly put his hand out, Tate tore the bill in half and handed one piece to him.

"What the hell is this?" the man demanded. "Some kind of stupid game?"

"No game," Tate assured him. "You get the other half of the hundred when I come back tomorrow and see for myself that she's all right." His eyes bored into the other man's dark ones. "We have a deal?"

The other man cursed roundly, then shoved his half of the bill into his pocket. "We have a deal," he retorted grudgingly.

"Good." Tate turned on his heel and crossed to the door.

Tate could almost feel Hannah's eyes watching him as he walked out of the suite.

Tomorrow seemed like an eternity away.

Chapter 2

"Did you see her? Was she there?"

Caleb Troyer fired the anxious questions at him the moment the thirty-one-year-old cabinetmaker walked into the makeshift, satellite FBI office.

Rather than the customary laid-back attitude normally associated with people who came from the Amish community, Caleb reminded him of a rocket that was ready to go off at the slightest provocation.

He couldn't say that he blamed the man, either.

"Yes, I saw her," Tate answered.

He glanced toward his sister, who'd come in with Caleb. He sincerely wished that Emma had followed protocol and persuaded Caleb to stay away and let the task force do its work.

Granted, the distraught man was Hannah's brother as well as Emma's fiancé. However, Caleb was also a civilian and, in his experience, overzealous, emotionally involved civilians had a way of causing a mission to fall apart.

They couldn't afford to have that happen. Too many young, innocent lives were at stake. And Tate had absolutely no intention of watching another mission self-destruct on him.

"How did she look?" Caleb pressed. "Have they…" At a loss, Caleb searched for a word that didn't drag a cat-o'-nine-tails across his soul, making it bleed when he considered the implication. "Have they *hurt* her in any way?" he finally asked nervously.

Beneath the cabinetmaker's apparent restlessness was anger. Tate could see it in the other man's gray eyes. Tall and muscular, Caleb Troyer, once unleashed, would be a force to be reckoned with. Not that he could honestly blame Caleb for what he was feeling. If all went well, maybe Caleb would get his chance at some payback when the operation was over.

But until then, the man had to be restrained.

"She looks tired and frightened," Tate told Hannah's brother.

His response was true—as far it went. What Tate didn't add was that when he'd initially seen Hannah in the motel room with the other two girls—before he'd been given the DVD to watch, she'd appeared to be drugged, as were the other girls. It was the easiest way to control the "inventory" and keep them from escaping.

Caleb definitely didn't need to know that. If he did, that might provide the missing ingredient that would set Hannah's brother off and God knew that Tate had more than enough to deal with without having to worry about the father of three suddenly going ballistic on him.

He could just picture Caleb storming into the motel

room, breaking down the door and subsequently getting shot for his efforts. If that happened, he'd have another body on his hands—as well as his conscience—and his sister to deal with.

Omitting certain details was the far safer way to go in this case.

"If you know where she is, then what are we waiting for?" Caleb demanded impatiently. He looked from Emma to Tate, searching for a glimmer of support. Why were they hanging back? "Let's go get Hannah and the other girls," he urged.

Turning on his heel, he was almost at the office door when Tate moved in front of him, blocking his way.

Tate completely sympathized with what the other man had to be going through, but what Caleb was proposing almost guaranteed a bloodbath.

"We can't just burst in there," he told Caleb as calmly as possible.

"Why not? Why can't we just walk into the place?" Caleb wanted to know. He didn't understand why this detective who'd promised to bring his sister and the other girls back was acting so reticent. Was he going back on his word? "You said there were just two godless thugs guarding the girls. There are three of us here— and you can get more," he pointed out.

Caleb was obviously focused only on rescuing Hannah at all costs. He didn't blame the man. But Tate was able to take several different points of view regarding the op besides the way Caleb did.

Tate did his best to make the other man understand. "Yes, I can get more manpower and maybe we could rescue Hannah and the other two without incident," he allowed, deliberately not going into how dangerous that sort of overt action could be. "But we also want to be able to rescue whatever other girls the ring has hidden away—the girls who were kidnapped for the same reason that your sister was taken. And we won't be able to do that if the guy who's the brains behind all this gets wind of what happened.

"The minute he does," Tate continued, "he'll go underground and those girls will be as good as dead. We'll never find them." Tate took a breath, searching the other man's face to see if his words had sunk in. Wondering if Caleb suspected that he was also lecturing himself as well as the victim's brother.

Lecturing himself because Tate had the exact same reaction, the exact desire as Caleb. He wanted to save Hannah and the girls with her as soon as possible. For two cents, he'd go in, guns blazing, and take down those two worthless pieces of trash guarding the girls with no more regret than he experienced stepping on a colony of ants.

Less.

The only problem was, right now there were only two henchmen visible and he knew damn well that there had to be more thugs involved than just Tweedledum and Tweedledee. An operation this big didn't function with just two flunkies.

There had to be more.

He put his hand on the Amish cabinetmaker's shoulder and looked at him compassionately.

"I know it's hard, but you're going to have to be patient," he told Caleb. "It's the only way we're going to be able to successfully rescue those girls. *All* of them," he emphasized.

Caleb nodded. It was obvious that he was struggling with himself. "You are right. We cannot just go in and rescue Hannah, not when there are other girls being held prisoner as well." And then he sighed and shook his head. "But this is hard," he complained.

Caleb would get no argument from him. "Nobody ever said it wouldn't be," Tate agreed. He looked at his watch. The handler should be getting the money right about now.

It was the handler whose job it was to pick up the funds from Gunnar that were needed for the exchange. At least that part was easy. Securing the funds would have been a great deal more difficult if he didn't have a billionaire brother who was willing to bring down this sex trafficking ring.

"So what's your next move?" Emma asked her brother as Caleb retreated to the far side of the room. There was tension in her voice.

"I've set up a private one-on-one session with Hannah," he told Emma. "Seems my credentials are so good that the man at the top is allowing me to have a private 'preview' with my future 'purchase.' I'm going to try to convince Hannah to trust me, but it's not going to be easy, given what she's been through."

Overhearing, Caleb looked up, suddenly alert. "Call her Blue Bird."

Tate exchanged quizzical looks with Emma. "What?" Tate asked.

"Call her Blue Bird," Caleb repeated, crossing back to them. "It was a nickname I gave Hannah when she was a little girl. She was always running around, fluttering about here and there, so full of life, of energy. One day when she seemed to be going like that for hours, I laughed and told her she was like one of the blue birds we saw in the spring. The comparison pleased her so I started calling her that. Blue Bird." A wave of memories assaulted him from all angles and he shook himself free, unable to deal with them right now. "If you call her that, she'll know you talked to me and she'll trust you."

Tate nodded. It was worth a shot. "Thanks. That'll help." As he switched his cell phone to vibrate, he saw the way Emma was frowning. "What's bothering you?"

There was a time she would have told him he was imagining things, that nothing was bothering her. But that was when the job was all important to her, and nothing came ahead of that. Now a lot of things did. And she was worried.

"Frankly, I don't like you walking back into the lion's den unarmed." She knew he was pushing his luck. "You made it out twice unharmed. The third time—" she began skeptically.

"Will be the charm," Tate assured her, finishing her sentence in a far different way than she'd intended to finish it.

But Emma continued to look unconvinced. "The people involved in this sex trafficking ring have already killed twice," she reminded him. "What's to stop them from killing you?"

He shrugged indifferently, as if she were worrying for no reason. "Well, for one thing, killing me off would be bad for business," he told her glibly. "They're after the money I told them I'd pay for Hannah. Word gets around that they've killed a client and their little virgins-to-the-highest-bidder scheme suffers a serious setback."

He put his hands on Emma's small shoulders. Funny, he never realized how fragile she could feel. Or how touched he could be by her concern. "Look, we've both been in law enforcement for a while now and nothing's ever happened to either of us, right?"

"That's my whole point," she insisted. She put one of her hands on top of his, silently bonding with him. "Our luck's bound to run out eventually."

"*Eventually* means someday—not today," he pointed out with conviction. "Now stop worrying—that's an order," he told her. "The sooner we get the information we need about whoever's pulling those strings, the sooner we get to wrap this up and Caleb over there gets to make an honest woman out of you."

Emma's mouth dropped open for a second, and then she shook her head. "I can't believe you just said that. Do you have any idea how incredibly old-fashioned that sounded?"

Her choice of words amused him. "You'd better get used to that, honey," Tate told her, kissing the top of his sister's head. "*Old-fashioned* goes with the bonnet and the butter churn."

Emma continued to look at him, a knowing look entering her eyes. She wasn't all that unusual, she thought. "Tell me you wouldn't give up everything for the right person if she came along."

"For the right person," he echoed, momentarily conceding the point, then quickly qualifying, "*If* she came along. But until she does, I've got work to do. And right now, I've got to pick up a suitcase full of money before those thugs get antsy and decide to turn Hannah over to another bidder."

The suitcase full of money meant he was seeing Hatfield, his handler. The thought of her brother walking around with that kind of money in a briefcase made her nervous. "I'll go with you," she volunteered.

But he had something else he felt was more important for her to do. "No, you stay here and make sure that your cabinetmaker doesn't decide to do something stupid and wind up breaking down the hotel suite door and hauling out one or both of those bozos."

Emma came to her fiancé's defense. "What would you do if someone kidnapped me?" Emma asked him pointedly, trying to make her brother see the situation from Caleb's point of view.

"Sending his next of kin a sympathy card comes to mind," Tate answered dryly. And then his smile faded for a moment as he gave her a serious answer. "I'd track the kidnapper to the ends of the earth and gut him seven ways to Sunday—" But he was trained to do that. It was different with Caleb. These were men they were talking about, not cabinets. "But we're not talking about me," he pointed out.

Emma shook her head as she laughed softly. "No, I guess we're not." She brushed a quick kiss against his cheek. She was going to worry until she saw him safe again. She couldn't help it. She was built that way.

"Watch your back, Big Brother," she told him.

"Always," he said. Crossing to the door, he opened it then paused for a moment to look at Hannah's brother. Lines of concern were etched deeply into his handsome, young face. "It's going to be all right," he promised the other man.

The expression on Caleb's face was half resigned, half hopeful.

It echoed perfectly the sentiment Tate felt within his soul.

The same two men he'd dealt with twice before were waiting for him in the hotel suite when he arrived with the briefcase of used hundred-dollar bills, arranged in nonsequential order, just as instructed.

The bald man with the goatee opened the door to

admit him before his knuckles could hit the door for a second time. Tate walked in, nodding at him and the equally bald African-American. On the latter, bald looked good. The same couldn't be said about the man with the goatee.

"It's all there," Tate told the African-American man eyeing the briefcase suspiciously as he placed it on the coffee table between the two men.

The man flipped both locks at the same time, then spared him a glance. "You don't mind if I see for myself, right?"

It was a rhetorical question. Nonetheless, Tate chose to answer it in his own way. He quickly pressed the lid back down in place before the other man could look inside. Tate met the guard's hostile gaze.

"I'd expect nothing less," Tate assured him.

"Then what the hell are you doing?" the guard demanded hotly.

Tate looked at the man with the goatee, then back at Waterford, the African-American. "I'm waiting for one of you to show me Jade."

"You've already seen her," Waterford snapped. "Twice."

"You're right," Tate agreed amicably. "And now I just want to make sure that she's actually here."

"He doesn't trust you, Nathan," the man with the goatee jeered.

"Shut up," Waterford ordered, obviously angry that his name had been used.

Tate pretended not to notice the flare-up. "Well, do I see her?" he wanted to know, still keeping the lid down. Tate could feel his biceps straining as he continued to hold the lid in place. It had turned into a contest of strength, one that Tate was determined to win.

Waterford did not take defeat easily. He looked as if he could snap a neck as easily as take in a deep breath.

"Bring her in," he instructed the other guard in the room.

The latter was angry at being ordered around like that in front of a relative stranger, but he was also obviously afraid to oppose the larger man. Muttering under his breath, the man with the mousy goatee went to the back of the suite, threw open the door leading into the bedroom and barked "Get out here" to the lone occupant in the bedroom.

A moment later, Hannah, her flame-red hair piled up high on her head, wearing a green gown that looked painted on, delicately glided into the sitting room.

Each time he saw her, Tate couldn't help thinking, she seemed even more beautiful than the last time. It almost made his soul ache to look at her, knowing what she had to have gone through. Was *still* going through, he amended.

He had a gut feeling that Hannah was tougher than she looked. He sincerely hoped so, for her sake.

"Satisfied?" the African-American barked, flinging his hand out and gesturing toward Hannah.

Tate withdrew his hand from the briefcase's lid. "Satisfied," he replied. Tate took a step back from the table. He smiled and nodded at Hannah before turning his attention to the man he'd made his bargain with the day before. Tate looked into his eyes, his gaze turning almost hypnotic. "And nobody touched her." It was both a question and a statement that waited to be confirmed.

"Nobody laid a damn finger on her—or anything else for that matter," the man with the goatee added when it was obvious that the client was waiting for more of a confirmation.

Tate looked at Hannah, who kept her gaze lowered, looking down at the rug. With the crook of his finger beneath her chin, he raised her head until she was looking directly at him.

"Is that true?" he asked her.

Surprised at being addressed directly without any curse words attached, a beat still passed before Hannah nodded her head.

"What are you asking her for?" the goatee demanded to know. "I said nobody touched her. I lived up to my half of the bargain," he declared impatiently. "Where's my money?"

"Right here," Tate said, placing the other half of the torn bill into the man's outstretched hand.

"What's that for?" Waterford wanted to know, eyeing the single torn section suspiciously.

"Insurance," was the unselfconscious reply. "Now I'd like some time alone with the girl."

"Sure, knock yourself out." The man with the goatee gestured toward the bedroom. "You paid for her, have at it," he urged, and then he leered, "Sure you don't want me to break her in for you?"

It was a crude play on words. Words that quickly faded away in the heat of the glare that had entered Tate's eyes.

"What I want," he began deliberately, "is for the two of you to make yourself scarce." Tate looked from one man to the other. Neither seemed to grasp what he was telling them, or made any attempt to leave the room. "You can stand guard in the hall outside the suite's door if it makes you happy."

"We're not leaving," the goatee growled.

"I'm not telling you to leave," Tate countered. "I'm telling you I want some privacy. There's only one way out of this suite and it's through that door." He deliberately pointed to it. "You can both stand guard in front of it, or take turns—I really don't care which you decide to do. But I don't want to feel crowded while I look over what a briefcase full of hundred-dollar bills just got me. Understand?" he demanded.

Waterford shook his head. "I don't know about this," he said skeptically.

"You're not leaving the hotel, just the room," Tate argued. "We'll still be right where you left us when you walk back in," he assured them, adding in a voice that brooked no nonsense, "Those are my terms. If you don't like them—" he made a move to reclaim the briefcase, his implication clear: he either got his way, or he would be *on* his way.

The choice was theirs.

The man with the goatee cursed roundly, adding a few disparaging words about having to put up with aggravating people.

In the end, he grudgingly said, "Okay, we'll be out in the hallway in front of the door. *Right in front* of the door," he emphasized. "So don't get any big ideas about making a break for it."

Tate deliberately looked at Hannah. "I assure you, any ideas I have have nothing remotely to do with the hotel door."

The men didn't look completely convinced, but they walked out of the suite. Once on the other side of the door, they made enough noise that just barely stopped short of waking the dead.

It was to let him know that they were right outside the door, as specified. Ready to stop him if he had any plans to escape with the girl.

Tate frowned. He didn't have time to think about those clowns right now. It was Hannah who commanded all his attention.

When he turned around to face her, he saw the fear in her eyes.

The real work, he knew, was still ahead of him.

Chapter 3

Finding herself alone with the stranger, Hannah did her best not to give in to the fear that had been her constant unwelcome companion since this terrible nightmare had begun.

It wasn't as if this man she was looking at was like the others she'd encountered in this world of outsiders. He seemed different than the two crude, insulting men who were in charge of keeping watch over her and the other girls who'd been abducted from her village and Ohio. Different even than Solomon Miller, a man who her small community had once turned out and who'd sought to avenge himself by throwing his lot in with the men who'd abducted her and the others.

This man she was with *seemed* different, Hannah silently reminded herself, but even she knew that appearances could be deceiving and she hadn't known

even a moment's kindness since she'd been torn away
from everything she knew and loved.

So why did she feel that this man somehow *was*
different?

The tips of her fingers felt like ice. Her whole body
felt as if it was alternating between hot and cold as she
struggled to keep fear from rampaging through her like
a runaway wild animal.

What was this man going to do to her?

And how could she stop him? He looked so much
more powerful than she was.

Her brain was still foggy from whatever it was that
the man with the facial hair had tried to force her to
swallow earlier. Foggy, but not completely useless because she'd managed to keep the drug hidden in the
corner of her mouth, between the inside of her lip and
her gum. Still, some of it had leached into her system.
But she'd heard enough to piece things together.

Even so, she couldn't really believe it. Didn't *want*
to believe what she'd heard through the door that separated this new, fancy prison from the outer room where
her jailers had sat, talking to the man who was now
towering over her.

Had she actually been *sold* to him?

It didn't seem possible.

People weren't sold to other people. Things like
that had taken place during a far more barbaric time,
a shameful passage in the country's history that was
mercifully a century and a half behind them.

People didn't *buy* people anymore. *They didn't.*

And yet…

And yet, she'd seen the briefcase before the lid had
come down on it. There'd been money in that case. A

great deal of money. Was that being exchanged for her? Had this man really *bought* her?

What did that *mean?*

Hannah could feel her soul seizing up within her as the fear she'd been trying so desperately to contain suddenly broke out of its confines and all but paralyzed her.

Maybe this was all just a horrible, horrible dream. A nightmare. And maybe, dear Lord, if she just closed her eyes, when she opened them again, she'd be back in her safe little house with her family around her. What she wouldn't give to hear the voices of her nieces, Katie, Ruthie and Grace—her brother Caleb's daughters—raised in some silly little inconsequential squabble.

Tears rose in Hannah's eyes and she fought to keep them back. She couldn't cry in front of this man, couldn't risk it. She'd seen the effect that tears had on these cruel beasts who'd ripped her world apart. Mary Yoder had cried and they'd beaten her for it, seeing tears as a sign of weakness.

She had no idea where Mary was now, or even if she was still alive.

These men who had become an unwanted daily part of her life had no respect for weakness, no compassion or even pity. They had nothing but contempt for its display, and if anything, when they encountered weakness, it just made them crueler.

She had to be strong, Hannah told herself. Only the strong survived and she needed to survive, needed to find a way to get back to her family again, back to Caleb, who needed her to help him take care of his motherless daughters.

Be strong, Hannah, be strong, she silently urged herself. *He knows Caleb. That has to mean something.*

Somehow, digging deep, Hannah found the strength

she was looking for. Found it and clung to it for all she was worth.

Raising her head, she forced herself to look into the tall, imposing stranger's eyes. They didn't look like the eyes of a cruel man. Perhaps she could talk him out of this shameful thing he was about to do.

"Please," she implored him. "You don't want to do this." Hannah took a deep breath, willing her nerves to remain steady. She congratulated herself on speaking without allowing a telltale tremor to emerge in her voice and betray her.

Her eyes remained fixed on the stranger's. Taking another breath, she repeated the sentence, her voice sounding a little stronger this time. "You don't want to do this."

The trouble was, God help him, he did, Tate thought. It wasn't that the undercover role he was playing had gotten to him. He found everything about this persona loathsome. Anyone who preyed on helpless girls, using money and connections to satisfy his unnatural lusts, was nothing short of despicable.

But the truth of it was, since the very first time he'd seen her face on that DVD recording that had contained a virtual catalog of innocence for would-be bidders to view, he'd found himself almost hopelessly attracted to the abducted young woman.

It didn't matter. He knew he couldn't do anything about it. Knew that to act in any way on these feelings under the pretext of playing his part was more than reprehensible. His sense of honor, or decency, wouldn't allow it.

But he couldn't be anything less than honest with himself and, the thing of it was, under different circumstances, he would have attempted to find a way to at least strike up a conversation with Hannah. Hopefully, that would lead to spending time with her and then perhaps…

Perhaps what? She was just twenty—and he wasn't. And hadn't been for a long time.

Besides, he reminded himself pointedly, *under any other circumstances, your paths wouldn't have even crossed.*

And it was true. When would a career detective have any occasion to meet a sheltered young woman who spent her whole life entrenched in the bosom of her close-knit Amish community? The answer to that was simple: never.

The tension in the room was so thick, he could almost *see* it. Somehow, he had to put Hannah at ease, make her relax a little by convincing her that he was *not* the enemy.

Tate took a step toward her and saw Hannah instinctively shrink back. The very action made him feel terrible for her.

I'm your friend, Hannah. Your friend.

But how did he get her to believe that? Especially since this room was undoubtedly bugged and probably under the ring's surveillance?

"Have they hurt you?" Tate asked her gently.

The young woman slowly moved her head from side to side, never taking her eyes off him, as if she was afraid that if she looked away, he would take the opportunity to jump her. It was painfully clear that she didn't trust him to maintain the small distance between them.

If she didn't trust him when it came to something so basic, how was he going to get her to trust him enough to tell him what he needed to know?

And then he recalled the nickname Caleb had told him to use. It was worth a try.

"You can tell me," he coaxed. "Did they hurt you, Blue Bird?" His voice deliberately dropped as he called her by the nickname.

Her gray-blue eyes widened and he heard Hannah's sharp intake of breath. She continued watching him as if she didn't know what to expect.

"Not since the last time you came," she finally replied, speaking so quietly that, had he not been looking at her lips, he wouldn't have even known that she'd answered.

So, the torn bill had worked, he thought. He didn't kid himself that the guard he'd given it to had any sense of honor, only greed, but that was all right. He wasn't above using whatever worked.

"But before then?" he pressed.

The small, perfect shoulders rose slightly and then lowered in an almost imperceptible shrug. The clinging green gown rustled a little.

"Before then," she murmured.

"Who?" he asked, moving closer to her.

Tate saw the young woman automatically shrink into herself again, but this time, she didn't step back the way she had before. This time, she remained where she was.

"The one with the scraggly hairs on his chin," she told him.

The man with the goatee, Tate thought. Of the two henchmen, he looked like the more dangerous one, the more unpredictable one.

"Did he hurt you…badly?" Tate pressed, unable to make himself ask Hannah if the scum had actually raped her.

Somehow, phrasing it that directly seemed to just

intensify the horror of the attack. He didn't want to resurrect painful memories for her, he just needed information.

To his relief, Hannah shook her head. "No, not badly." She knew what he was asking her. Uncomfortable, she pressed her lips together, testing each word cautiously as she uttered it. Her eyes were once again riveted on his face as she watched his reaction. "He tried, but the other man—" What was it that she'd heard the dark-skinned man called? "Nathan," she suddenly remembered. "Nathan pulled him off me and hit him. Nathan said that no one would pay for me if I was ruined." She raised her head, a glimmer of defiance in her eyes, as if these were odds she'd managed somehow to beat. "You paid for me."

Tate paused. He had no doubt that there was probably a camera in the suite somewhere—possibly several—watching his every move, recording his every word. Anything he wanted to convey to her would have to be almost inaudible if he wanted to have a prayer of getting out of here alive—and ever coming back to rescue the girls.

"Yes," he answered. "I paid for you. Or at least made a partial payment," he qualified. The rest he was to bring to the "party" that was being given. A party where he and other so-called pillars of society were to be coupled with their bought-and-paid-for virgins.

A party that, rumor had it, the mastermind behind this ring was also to attend.

She didn't quite follow him. A partial payment? "So do you own me?" she asked, still unable to grasp the concept, even as she heard herself ask the question.

"I will as soon as I make the second payment," he corrected her, playing to whatever audience would eventually be sitting on the other side of the camera and observing this.

Hannah paused, her head spinning. The conversation didn't seem real to her, like something in one of the books that were forbidden for her and young people like her in the village to read.

"And when you make that second payment," she finally said, "then what?"

"Then you're mine," he said as matter-of-factly as he could. He saw another glimmer of defiance in her eyes before it faded away again.

Good for you, Tate thought, pleased. They hadn't broken her spirit. This meant he had something to work with. And that, hopefully, would help her get back to normal once he brought her back to her village.

Watching him intently, Hannah was frantically searching for something to cling to, something to give her hope that there would be an end to this nightmare and that the end she was seeking wasn't tied to her demise.

There *had* to be more to this than what there was on the surface.

There had to be, she silently insisted.

"Why did you call me what you did earlier?" she wanted to know, focusing on the name the stranger had used. How could he have possibly known she'd been called that as a child?

Unless…

Unless he *had* actually spoken to Caleb. Had Caleb sent him, as the man had claimed? It didn't seem possible. Caleb wouldn't have left Paradise and walked among the outsiders—

He would. For me, she realized and knew it was true. Hannah looked at the stranger expectantly, waiting for an answer. Then, in case he'd forgotten what she'd asked, she said, "You called me Blue Bird."

"Blue Birds look pretty against the sky when they soar," he said evasively, doing his best to recall exactly how Caleb had explained the reason for the nickname to him. "It just seemed to fit you," he concluded, looking at her pointedly.

Willing her to make the connection between the nickname and what he'd whispered to her the last time he'd seen her.

Had she heard him then?

Or had she been too drugged or too despondent at the time to understand what he was saying to her?

Tate watched the young woman's face for some sort of clue. Unlike his own stoic expression—his "game" face—Tate saw a myriad of emotions wash over Hannah's heart-shaped face.

And then, he could have sworn that what looked like enlightenment entered her eyes—just before she shut down again. Shut down as if she was afraid to believe him. Afraid to get her hopes up, for fear that she was only going to have them dashed again.

"You don't have to be afraid," he said to her as gently as he dared. "I'm not going to do anything to you. I just want to talk."

"Talk?" she echoed, as if she didn't understand the word. As if it was just too much for her to hope for.

"Talk," he repeated. "I want to get to know you."

She still looked as if she didn't comprehend the word, or at least was confused by it. "They said…" The words felt as if they had gotten stuck in her throat and she tried again. "They said I should be 'nice' to you."

There was no mistaking what the euphemism actually meant, though she refused to think about it.

"Who's *they?*" Tate asked, doing his best not to put any undue emphasis on the question. He wanted it to sound like nothing more than an idle query, one of many that could crop up in the course of a conversation. "Do you mean the two men outside the door?" he asked, trying to get her to talk to him.

She shook her head. "No, another man. I'd never seen him before. He and the man with him said if I wasn't nice to you, I'd be sorry." Either way, she lost, Hannah thought.

Picking up the slender thread, Tate continued, doing his best to sound almost uninterested, just mildly curious. "This man you didn't know, did you hear anyone address him by name?"

But Hannah shook her head again. "They just called him 'Boss,'" she told him.

Jackpot!

Kind of.

Subduing his excitement, Tate lowered his voice and asked, "What did he look like?"

Instead of answering him, Tate saw apprehension return to her eyes as she looked at him nervously. "You are trying to trick me." It was half a question, half a statement.

"Trick you?" he echoed in surprise. Why would she think that?

"Yes," Hannah insisted. "You are here. He is the man who arranges these things. You must know what he looks like." Suspicion rose in her voice. Was he trying to trap her somehow? She didn't understand any of this, not the abduction, not why she had to be here, nothing. "Why are you doing this to me?"

"I'm not trying to trick you," he assured her gently. "And the only men that I've dealt with are those two gorillas outside in the hall. Them, and that man I first spoke to on the telephone," he added.

The first step in the operation had been finding the website. The one that had advertised "a cleaning service that will leave you swearing that you've never been serviced so well in your life." It had fairly *screamed* sex trafficking. Tate was almost certain that the voice he'd heard when he dialed the number had belonged to the man in charge. And that *that* man wasn't just some ingenious nobody off the street. Rumors and suspicions pointed to the head man being someone high up, not just on this food chain, but on the social food chain as well.

Someone with dark secrets and a darker soul, who satisfied perversions that made anything Tate had previously come up against seem almost docile and childlike by comparison.

Tate looked down into Hannah's face. Right now, she was the closest he'd gotten to this sex trafficking ring. She might even unknowingly hold the key to taking it down. He needed to find out what she knew. The only way to do that was to talk to her. But he needed to make certain that he wasn't overheard; otherwise, the op fell apart and the whole ring could just disappear into the night, taking the girls with it—or, if that was too much trouble, leaving behind their lifeless bodies. He had a feeling that it could go either way, and that was a risk he wasn't about to take.

Debating what to do, after a beat Tate took her hand in his and led her over to the sofa. It was obvious that she followed him reluctantly, but he could work with that, he told himself.

When he turned to look at her, the apprehensive expression he saw on Hannah's face almost tore him apart. He'd always thought of himself as a protector, a man women felt safe with. To see himself reflected as a potential monster in Hannah's eyes was a startling revelation. But there was no other way he could interpret what he saw. Hannah looked as if she was holding her breath, waiting for something terrible to happen to her.

Tate forced himself to continue. He was her only chance at survival—he had to remember that. Sitting down, Tate tugged lightly on her hand. When she looked at him quizzically, he coaxed, "Come sit on my lap."

Her mouth went completely dry.

Was this how it was to begin? The destruction of her virginity—was it going to start with a softly spoken invitation, only to escalate to unspeakable behavior?

She wanted to run.

And yet, she knew she had no choice. Nathan and the other man were just outside the door. She wouldn't make it past the threshold. And she didn't want to die the way her friends had. She wanted to live. To live and someday find a way to escape.

So, when the man who had paid for her tugged on her hand again, Hannah willed her knees to bend and did what he bade her to.

She sat down on his lap.

She was trembling, Tate realized the moment she made contact with his lap. He could feel her trembling and hated the fact that she was afraid of him.

Hated this whole charade.

But he knew it was the only way to save Hannah and all the other girls who had been so viciously snatched away from their families, not to mention everything they knew. And their only sin was that they were all so innocent in a world where innocence had ceased to be a common thing and was now a rarity, something to be elevated and observed, like a perfectly cut diamond.

He had no choice but to continue playing this role he had swiftly come to despise.

Tate slipped one arm around her waist, holding Hannah against him. Inclining his head, he began to slowly kiss the nape of her neck.

He struggled to keep from immersing himself in the scent, the feel, the taste, of her.

It's a part—you're just playing a part, he silently insisted as he lectured himself over and over again not to get caught up in what he was doing.

Despite everything, despite his desperate attempt to keep a tight rein on himself, Tate could feel his body responding to Hannah. Responding to the intoxicating, sweet taste of her skin against his lips.

Dammit, get a grip, Colton. You're supposed to be here to rescue her, not ravage her or scare the poor girl to death. She's not your private playground.

Satisfied that he had performed as expected for whatever camera or cameras hidden in the room for the sole purpose of observing his every move, Tate whispered the same message into Hannah's ear that he'd told her yesterday.

Except that he embellished on it.

"My name is Tate. Caleb sent me. He was the one who told me to call you Blue Bird so that you'd know I was telling you the truth. I'm here to rescue you," he told her, his arms tightening just a touch around her waist to prevent any sudden moves on her part, motivated by surprise.

He couldn't let his guard down, not even for a moment. "You and the others," he added. His breath feathered along the side of her neck as he spoke. "But this isn't going to be easy and I'm going to need your help to pull it off."

Hannah turned her head slowly to look at him. He could tell by the look in her eyes that he'd made a breakthrough.

She was finally beginning to believe him.

Chapter 4

Hannah continued to look at the tall stranger, doing her best not to appear as startled as she suddenly was. Startled *and affected*. His breath had rippled along her neck when he spoke to her.

Heaven help her, but she'd *felt* something then, although she wasn't sure just what.

She'd been so afraid of lowering her guard, so focused on trying to remain as alert and vigilant as possible in order to resist being abused, that she'd all but turned into a brick wall.

But this man who claimed to have been sent by her brother—he'd created the tiniest hairline crack in the wall that she'd erected around herself. And because of that crack, she'd *experienced* something.

Something other than fear.

Was that his plan?

Was he trying to trick her into lowering her guard,

even just a little? Was he trying to make her believe that she was on the cusp of being rescued only so that he could take what he wanted without going through the trouble of having to physically fight with her?

Her friends had resisted and they were dead now. But she knew that small in stature though she was, she was actually physically stronger than they had been. And she was more persuasive than they had been. She'd been listening to the conversations around her. Listening and learning.

She looked into the stranger's eyes, trying to decide if he was who he said he was—someone sent by Caleb—or if he was just being clever, piecing together information he might have been told by whoever had put her virtue up for auction.

The stranger's eyes were aqua, a distinctive shade she'd never seen before. Was that a sign of some sort, that he was special, *different* from the others who pawed her friends with heavy hands?

Or was she creating "proof" where there was none to be had?

Hannah let out a slow, shaky breath. She would risk it. She would believe him. "What can I do?" she asked quietly.

Her question could be interpreted many ways, Tate assured himself, acutely aware that she'd voiced it loudly enough to be picked up by the camera. One way to see it was to believe she had resigned herself to her fate and in order to avoid being beaten for appearing to resist, she was offering to do whatever it took to comply with this role she was forced to play.

Do whatever he wanted her to do. All he had to do was tell her.

At least that was the way he hoped the goons who were watching this would see it.

Drawing Hannah even closer to him so that his cheek was against hers, Tate whispered, "Do you know the head man's name?"

There it was again, that warmth along her skin, that corresponding ripple within the pit of her stomach—or at least the general vicinity, she amended.

Hannah looked uneasily at this man who held her body on his lap and her fate in his hands.

What *was* it that he was doing to her? Where were these strange sensations coming from? She had questions, frustrating questions, and no visible way to address any of them.

In response to his question about the man who had to be in charge of all this, she shook her head. But before she could open her mouth to testify to her ignorance, he surprised her. He took hold of her chin in his hand. Then, as she watched, her breath caught in her throat, the man who had exchanged a briefcase full of money to purchase some time with her lowered his mouth to hers and lightly brushed his lips over it.

Just before his lips made contact with hers, she thought she heard him murmur, "Whisper it into my ear."

If she was going to ask "What?" she never had the opportunity, because that was when he kissed her.

And everything changed from that moment on.

She had been kissed before. One of the boys in her school had stolen a kiss from her once, then run off, afraid of being caught. She remembered thinking, as he ran away, that it was a very strange custom, rubbing skin on skin. She'd felt curious as to why he'd done it, but couldn't remember feeling anything beyond that.

The incident wasn't repeated, possibly because the boys in her village were afraid of Caleb, who was her protector.

This, however, was different.

Very different.

Hannah knew why this man was doing what he did—at least, she knew what he'd intimated his reason for taking this route was. He wanted to exchange information with her without anyone overhearing or suspecting what was really happening.

But if that was the case, was she supposed to feel this in response?

And what *was* this that she was feeling?

She had no name for it, no frame of reference, other than that time the water had been too hot for her when she was bathing and it had created a corresponding, almost unbearable warmth all over her, both without and within.

Drawing his head back now, Tate looked at her, waiting for Hannah to comply with his barely audible instruction. Doing his best to harness the hammering of his heart, which was pounding in direct response to kissing her.

Damn, he was going to have to watch himself. It was too easy to allow the lines between his roles to blur, to throw himself into the part of a man who'd just bought himself a preview of the night of uniquely exquisite passion he was being promised.

Hannah, in her innocence, was getting to him and he couldn't allow that. Distracted cops made mistakes. Fatal mistakes.

"Go on," he coaxed out loud, acting like a teacher waiting for his student to demonstrate what she'd just learned.

She was shaking again, at least she was inside, Hannah thought as she leaned over in slow motion, her lips feathering along his skin just below his ear.

"I don't know," she whispered. "I never heard anyone call him by name."

Tate's stomach muscles tightened so hard, he would have sworn on a stack of Bibles that his gut had suddenly been tied into a huge, unworkable knot.

Cupping her face in his hands, he brought his mouth down to Hannah's again, then lightly rained gentle, tightly controlled kisses along her cheek, working his way to the other ear.

"Can you describe him?" he wanted to know. They had a name, Seth Maddox, but it never hurt to verify that their source hadn't just been selling them a bill of goods.

Her breath was growing increasingly shorter, even as she felt her pulse accelerating. And her head was beginning to spin again, just the way it had when she'd been forced to drink that awful-tasting liquid. The one that robbed her of her ability to think, to differentiate shapes and people.

Leaning in against him again, she tried to imitate what he'd just done. But when she kissed him this time, she forgot to move on.

At least, she did for a long moment.

Instead, holding his face in her hands the way he had done with hers, her lips pressing against his, Hannah realized that she was lingering. Lingering—and enjoying it.

Was that pleasure she was feeling?

How *could* it be?

What was happening—all of this—was against her will. Or at least it had begun that way when the door had closed behind those henchmen, locking her in with this man.

Again she wondered if he was just pretending to be here to save her so that she wouldn't struggle when he finally had his way with her.

But he'd used her nickname, she reminded herself. He'd called her Blue Bird.

Her thoughts felt as if they were going in two directions at the same time. Her head ached.

Only Caleb knew about that name or used it.

Only Caleb and his girls, she amended.

His daughters had heard him call her that more than once. But Ruthie, Grace and Katie had no occasion to tell anyone else, she silently argued.

She raised her eyes to the stranger. So did she trust him—or not?

Hannah felt horribly confused.

He was waiting, she realized. Waiting for her to tell him something. He was waiting for her to give him the man's description, she suddenly remembered, struggling to clear her head.

Her lips lightly brushed against his cheek. At the same time, she whispered, "Older than you. Shorter. Thinner. Silver in his black hair. Perhaps fifty, perhaps younger." She raised her eyes to his, feeling as if she'd failed him. Failed her fellow sisters being held captive as well.

"I'm sorry I'm not a help," she apologized. The words of regret almost choked her.

"Nothing to be sorry about," he assured her, measuring out each word slowly, tailoring his words to the role he was playing. It had to be in keeping with the facade he had put into place. "You did very well."

She didn't see how she could have.

Hannah searched the stranger's face and saw that he was serious. She shook her head in response, but said nothing. Not until he gently slid her off his lap and helped her back up to her feet, getting up with her.

It was time to go. Before he forgot his training, did something incredibly stupid and blew the whole mission, not to mention his cover.

"I'll be in touch," he promised.

For the second time in ten minutes, Hannah's breath stopped in her throat. But this time, it was fear that created that sensation.

Her eyes were only a shade smaller than saucers. "You're leaving?" she asked.

Tate inclined his head ever so slightly. "I have to."

Because he'd gone to so much trouble to mask both his words and hers, she emulated his actions. She could see that she had surprised him when she pulled her torso up against him.

In a barely perceptible whisper, she entreated, "Take me with you."

When she added the word *please,* Tate thought his very heart would break right then and there. He would have given ten years of his life to be able to comply, to do exactly as she asked.

But he couldn't.

He had to keep the bigger picture in mind and the bigger picture involved rescuing not just Hannah, but all the other girls who had been yanked out of their homes and their schools, dehumanized, drugged and dragged here, to be offered as tantalizing pieces of flesh to men whose souls were blacker than the bottom of an abyss.

So, though he hated himself for refusing her, for forcing her to remain here another moment, Tate took hold of her shoulders and held her in place as he told her words he knew she did *not* want to hear: "I can't."

He saw disbelief, horror and desperation play over her exquisitely formed face.

"Yes, you can," she insisted, angry tears gathering in her eyes. "You can take my hand and walk out of here with me. You said you *bought* me. You gave them all that money for me."

Had it all been a lie, after all? Had he just been toying with her, making her believe there was an end in sight when there really wasn't?

But why?

It didn't make any sense to her.

"That was to show good faith," he explained.

Anyone listening to this exchange would see this as just a confrontation between a john and the unhappy object of his obsession—nothing more, he thought. It would stand to reason that she would be desperate to escape and willing to do whatever it took to make it happen.

"So I can get invited back to the party," he added, trying to make her understand why his hands were tied at the moment. Hoping that she could forgive him.

"Party?" she echoed. The word had an ominous sound to it. "What sort of a party?"

She didn't know, he realized. They really were keeping the girls in the dark. "For the organization's prospective clients—and other girls like you," he explained carefully.

Her mouth went dry again. More men meant more of a chance that someone else would claim her.

"So they can—they can—" She stumbled, unable to make herself form the words that described the ravaging that she felt certain would take place.

Tate placed his finger over her lips, silencing her. He didn't want her saying any more, didn't want her thinking about anything except that she *would* be rescued. Just not today.

The look in her eyes was clearly conflicted, but he forced himself to meet it. If he looked away, she'd think he was lying to lull her into a false sense of security and the exact opposite would happen.

"I'll be back for you," he promised. It was an oath, a vow he meant to keep no matter what it took.

Anyone overhearing would think it was just a wealthy john telling his "escort" of choice that he wasn't through with her, Tate told himself.

But he fervently hoped that Hannah would see beyond the obvious and realize he was making a commitment to her, a promise that he was going to return and rescue her as well as the others.

Because he was.

Hannah pressed her lips together. The wariness he'd seen in her eyes earlier returned. As did the apprehensive air.

She didn't fully trust him, he thought. How could he blame her? He'd given her a catchphrase, a nickname, and then turned her down when she asked him to get her out of here because she was clearly afraid of remaining here another moment. In her place, he'd have trust issues, too.

"When?" she finally asked.

Maybe there was a part of her that *did* believe him. At least he could hope. "Soon," he told her with as much feeling as he dared. "Very soon."

Just as the words were out of his mouth the door to the suite flew open and the two guards he'd relegated to the hallway came back inside.

He'd been right to assume that there were hidden cameras in the rooms and that the duo had been watching their every movement the entire time. Better careful than sorry—and dead, he told himself.

The man with the scraggly excuse for a goatee looked as if he could be outsmarted by a semi-intelligent raccoon. But the other, more powerful-looking one, Nathan, might be a real problem to them if he was so inclined.

Tate wanted the odds to be more on his side before he risked Hannah's life in an escape attempt. The sting would be a far more favorable occasion for things to go down.

If the wait didn't kill him.

"You about done?" the goateed man asked. Deep-set, marblelike eyes slid from him to Hannah.

Tate *really* didn't like the way the scum was looking at Hannah.

"Yes, I am," Tate replied calmly, his tone once again belying the churning emotions that were swirling dangerously just beneath the surface.

He could easily envision himself smashing that smirking, annoying face dead center with his fist. He was really going to enjoy taking these people down, he thought. Enjoy it the way he hadn't enjoyed anything in a long, long time.

"When will I receive my invitation to the party?" he asked, making certain that his question was addressed to both men.

He was well aware of the danger of openly favoring one henchman over the other at this point.

Pitting them against each other had its place and its benefits, but not yet. That was a card to be played closer to the end.

"When the boss is satisfied," the Scraggly Goatee answered condescendingly.

Tate kept his hands at his sides, but he curled his fingers into fists, wishing he was free to act on impulse rather than orders and protocol. He could take both men easily, even though they had guns and he didn't. He was trained for that sort of thing, using surprise and skills to his advantage. He could even make a clean getaway with Hannah if he timed it just right—but it would be at the cost of all those other lives. The abducted girls would be forever lost to their families, swallowed up without a trace.

So he remained immobile, telling himself it was all for the greater good.

Nathan eyed Tate with more than a little contempt in his eyes before he answered. "Keep your cell handy. You'll get a call soon. Within the next few hours," he added.

Tate nodded. "Thanks."

A noise behind him made him look over his shoulder. The man with the bad goatee hustled a weary-looking Hannah back into the bedroom again. He raised his voice so that the henchman knew he was talking to him.

"The deal's off if she's hurt in any way." That was so neither of them would feel free to strike her where her injuries would be initially covered up by clothing.

Looking on, Waterford appeared to be somewhat amused.

"You really like this one, huh?" he asked. As if he'd already had his answer, Nathan shook his bald head, bemused. "Don't really see why," he confessed. "One pretty much seems like another. Cover up their faces and you can't tell the difference."

Tate paused by the door. It was a very narrow line

he was walking and he knew it. One misstep and he would go headfirst into the lion's den, to be ripped apart and devoured.

But he wanted to be sure that nothing happened to Hannah in any way between now and whenever the so-called "party" was going to take place. After that, they were going to be home free.

Because the sting was set to go down at the same time.

He looked at Waterford pointedly, his message clear. "I'm not planning on covering her face," he told the muscular man.

He was surprised to hear Waterford laugh in response. The man looked almost human as he shrugged his wide shoulders and said, "Every man's got his own thing, I guess."

Tate couldn't imagine what Waterford's "thing" was, but he was fairly certain that he didn't want to stick around to find out. The only thing he wanted was for this operation to be over—successfully over—so that he could bring Hannah back to the people who were waiting for her. Back to her family.

If, at the same time, the thought generated an odd emptiness within him, well, he didn't have any time to try to explore that or figure out why he felt that way. There was much too much to do in the next few hours. He had a sting to finalize. And more money to get from Gunnar to use as bait. Greed had a way of escalating and the price that had been agreed to at the first auction was most likely suffering from growing pains because it had been increased.

He wasn't about to lose this opportunity—or have the sting go bad—because of something as insignificant as not being able to come up with enough funds to pull it off.

He hurried down the hall to the bank of elevators and punched the down button.

The next few hours were going to be crucial. For all of them, he couldn't help thinking, looking over his shoulder down the corridor toward the hotel suite he'd just left.

And envisioning the girl inside who was waiting to be rescued.

"I'll come back for you," he whispered again under his breath.

Chapter 5

"You've earned an invitation to the party," the cold, steely voice on the other end of the line said to Tate later that same evening. The call had come in on the cell phone that was exclusively registered to his "Ted Conrad" persona.

Tired after his long day, Tate nonetheless was instantly alert. He'd been waiting for the call—and, his gut told him, to hear from this specific man—since he had walked away from that tenth-floor hotel room earlier today.

Still, there was a game to play and to win, and Tate knew that he had to play it well. He feigned confusion. "Who is this?" he asked sharply.

"Why, the facilitator of your dreams, Mr. Conrad, who else?" the cold voice replied. The laugh that followed was all but frost-coated. It was obvious that the man on the other end of the line was enjoying the cat-

and-mouse game, secure in the knowledge that he was in control. "I must say, Mr. Conrad, for a man I've never heard of until just recently, your background has turned out to be truly impressive."

The background the caller was referring to had been created and entrenched in the right places thanks to his handler and the small crew he worked with who knew how to plant detailed information in files thought to be absolutely above hacking.

Even so, suspicion was never far away and always within reach. Because of that, Tate wondered now if the man on the other end of the call was on the level or mocking him.

If it was the latter, then he would have to be alert for some kind of a setup. This party he'd just been vetted for—did attending mean that he would be walking into a trap?

Tate's natural instincts warned him to proceed with caution, but they were also short on time. He couldn't afford to be overly wary in the name of self-preservation. There was a great deal at stake and this could very well be their one and only chance to rescue the girls and catch the main players in this sex trafficking ring. He couldn't drag his feet, but that still didn't make his uneasy feeling go away.

Tate supposed that if he wasn't so suspicious, most likely he would have been dead by now. Overconfident people were careless and being careless almost always got you killed.

"Maybe I haven't heard of you, either," Tate countered loftily, curious to hear what the man would say. The caller clearly had a large ego and that could only work in the investigation's favor, Tate thought.

For a second time, he heard the man on the other

end laugh. The sound was short, oddly cruel and completely dismissive.

"If that was an attempt to get me to blurt out my name, Mr. Conrad, you'll have to do better than that— if I were inclined to keep it secret. Which I'm not," he continued after a pause, as if he were playing out a fishing line. "Not to worry, Mr. Conrad. All will be revealed Friday night," the man promised ominously.

Okay, he was right, Tate thought. The man was definitely mocking him. Moreover, the man was clearly secure in what he perceived to be his superiority.

"Why then?" Tate wanted to know.

"All these questions," the voice mocked. For a second, Tate thought the man would hang up. But instead, he went on to answer the question. "Because after Friday's party, I will have enough on you to destroy you if I wanted to. Call it insurance."

Tate could swear he felt the man's fangs going into his neck. Thanks to his sources, he had a more than reasonable idea, although still not confirmed, of the identity of the scumbag he was talking to. Most likely, the man on the other end was Seth Maddox, a high-profile millionaire in New York City who'd made his fortune thanks to his astute investment acumen. Maddox more than fit the profile that had been put together regarding the man who was running the sex trafficking ring.

"Then this is a stalemate," Tate acknowledged.

"An equal balance of power," the man corrected. "Of course, if you'd rather opt out—" he offered loftily. His very tone said he knew there wasn't a chance in hell that would happen.

If possible, Tate's contempt for the man who was pulling all the strings behind this operation increased. "Where and when?" Tate asked, curbing his impatience.

The laugh was even more irritating this time around. It literally dripped of smugness. "So, we're still on. Good. Friday at 11:30 p.m. at the old abandoned Hubbard Warehouse just outside of North Philly." There was a brief pause, then the man asked, "You're familiar with it?"

The building sounded vaguely familiar, although he couldn't place it. But even as they spoke, the location was being plotted by one of his team. "I can find it," Tate assured the caller.

The moment the words were out, Tate remembered. The warehouse had once belonged to a thriving toy manufacturer. But when the company's target audience turned its attention toward video games, the toy manufacturer closed up shop. Hubbard's Toys disappeared from toy stores and, eventually, the warehouse was stripped bare, now housing rats rather than children's dreams.

"Good. I look forward to finally meeting you. I know I don't have to tell you to come alone." The warning in the voice was enough to send chills down the spine of a hardened criminal.

"Just me and my money," Tate replied. He was rewarded with what sounded like an actual chuckle, this time devoid of frost.

The next moment, it was gone.

"All the company a man could ask for" was the mastermind's approving response. "Except, perhaps, for a young, untried innocent. Don't be late. Doors close at midnight. After that—I don't care who you are—you won't get in."

Was the man concerned about the police or was this just a ploy to sound even more exclusive? Tate had a feeling it was most likely the latter. But he had a more pressing question on his mind.

"And Jade will be there?"

He had to ask. The man he was talking to was perverse enough to sequester her somewhere else just to keep him twisting in the wind—and returning for the next go-round, whenever that might be.

There wasn't going to be another go-round, Tate thought. *Not if I can help it.*

"Heart still set on that one, eh?" the voice mocked.

In this case, there was nothing to be gained by pretending he was indifferent to who he "received" in exchange for the briefcase full of money.

"Yes, it is."

The mastermind's response surprised Tate. "I like a man who knows what he wants. Yes, Jade will be there, ready to do whatever you want her to," the man added. "She knows damn well what'll happen to her if she doesn't."

Undoubtedly that was supposed to impress him, Tate thought, disgusted. He found it hard keeping his mouth shut and refraining from telling this subhuman how he would have loved to be given an excuse to gut him the way he deserved.

But there was nothing to be gained by that—or by torturing himself with the knowledge that his hands were absolutely tied right now and would continue to be until this was all resolved the *right* way.

He was damn glad that the sting was going down soon. He wasn't sure how much of this man he was going to be able to take. His blood ran cold when he started to think of what could have happened to Hannah, as well as the others, had Solomon Miller not come to them asking to trade information for immunity.

Without him, Emma and Caleb would have never found the bodies of those poor murdered girls and he wouldn't have known about the upcoming "party," where bored or depraved wealthy men were allowed to act out fantasies best revealed on a psychiatrist's couch.

"See you tomorrow night," the man on the other end said. Even that sounded mocking. And then the connection was terminated.

The second the call was over, Emma came into the hotel room, which was far less upscale than the one where he'd met with Hannah and her guards. His sister shook her head, telling him what he already suspected. The call wasn't traceable.

"It was a disposable cell," she said. "Randall couldn't pin down a signal," she added, referring to the computer whiz attached to their team.

Tate wasn't surprised. Despite the two goons at the hotel, he was certain these weren't amateurs they were dealing with. If they had been, the ring would have been history by now, instead of the elusive threat that it was. With any luck, though, that would all change after tomorrow night.

"We got Miller to confirm what we already suspected," Emma continued, taking a seat for a moment on the edge of the bed. "You were talking to Seth Maddox."

Well, that did fit what he'd heard about the man. Maddox was a risk taker who played for high stakes because he enjoyed the rush of the risk and the thrill of winning. He also wasn't above playing dirty to reach his goal.

"Have you got a voice match to confirm yet?" he wanted to know. There was always the chance that

Miller was lying to throw them off, playing both sides against the middle.

"Randall's working on it," she told him. "Should have it any minute now." She laughed then and saw her brother raise a quizzical eyebrow. She let him in on the joke. "I think Miller's insulted that we're not taking his word for it."

They needed more than hearsay to secure the warrants that they were going to need. A voice match was going to be part of the evidence. Besides, he had a feeling they were going to need all the help they could get.

"Right now, the sensitive feelings of a confidential informant aren't exactly high on my list of concerns," Tate told his sister. In his mind, he replayed his words to the man on the phone. "I'm going to need another briefcase," he told his sister.

Emma grinned. "I suppose you're going to want money in it."

He laughed shortly. "Well, yeah, that's the general idea."

"Can't get by on your good looks?" she asked, amused.

"Maybe next time," he answered dryly. "In the meantime, I need that briefcase crammed to the locks with money."

Money to supposedly buy an entire evening of ecstasy with a virgin of his choice. From the intel they had picked up so far, he was going to be in the company of politicians, athletes, Hollywood movers and shakers, not to mention renowned Wall Street investors. All well known, all powerful men.

And all depraved.

Tate felt as if he needed to take a shower already.

"Gunnar has taken care of it," Emma assured him seriously.

The pieces were all coming together, Tate thought as he nodded.

"You up for this?" Emma asked her brother the following evening.

Tate was dressed in a designer suit that appeared to have been hand-tailored just for him. He cut a handsome figure, Emma thought proudly. But pride took a backseat to concern. Of late, she had become more and more aware of the body count and she couldn't help being worried about him.

"You're going to be all alone in a tank of piranhas," she reminded him.

He saw the concern in his sister's eyes and thought of all the times they'd fought as children. But, fighting or not, there'd always been an undercurrent of love there. Their adoptive parents had seen to that. He doubted if he and his siblings could have been closer if they *had* shared the same bloodlines.

"Yeah, but knowing there's a SWAT team, not to mention you, right outside, ready to rush the place, will make me feel bulletproof," he said, trying to get Emma to focus on the manpower that was backing him up. It was practically a squadron. That should make her feel better about this. "How about you, Tomato-head?" he asked her, deftly changing the topic. "How does it feel knowing this is your last assignment?"

She wasn't focusing on anything except the next step in the plan. "Ask me after we get them," Emma told him. She placed the suitcase in front of him on the bed and snapped the locks open.

"I'll do that." Tate lifted the lid and glanced at the

sea of green. "All there," he murmured more to himself than to Emma.

"By the way, I forgot to tell you. Randall confirmed the voice patterns," she told Tate. "You were talking to Seth Maddox, all right. Guess being a millionaire NYC investor, rolling in cash, just wasn't enough for the man."

"No satisfying some men," Tate quipped dryly, shaking his head. He took a deep breath, bracing himself. The next moment, he was surprised by Emma, who threw her arms around his neck and hugged him. "Hey, what's this?" he asked.

"For luck," she answered, then backed off self-consciously.

"Since when do we need luck?" he teased her. "We're Coltons, remember? We make our own luck." He snapped the locks back into place, then picked up the suitcase. "Okay, let's get this show on the road," he urged and led the way out of the hotel room.

The cars that were parked outside the abandoned warehouse that evening would have made an automobile enthusiast's mouth water. There had to be over twenty of them and, Tate observed, not a single economy model in the lot.

He wasn't much on cars himself. If it had four wheels and was reliable, that was good enough for him. But he had to admit that the BMWs, Mercedes and Ferraris, not to mention a host of other high-end vehicles, were an impressive sight, especially when they were all in one place, the way they were tonight. He had driven over in a Ferrari. Part of the act. He'd parked the car next to a Bentley and gotten out.

He saw no one in the shadows, but knew his people were there. They were good at being invisible.

Tate talked to them now, taking advantage of the two-way amplifier he had hidden deep in his right ear.

"You'd think people who were lucky enough to afford wheels like that without blinking would be happy with their lot instead of trolling the internet, looking to get their thrills by ruining innocent young girls," he murmured to the people he knew were listening.

"No justice," he heard Emma answer.

"Sure there is. It's us," he said just before he terminated any further exchange.

He was drawing too close to the entrance to be seen murmuring to himself. This had to go off without a hitch in order to ensure that no one would be hurt. At least, no one who mattered, he amended, thinking of Hannah and the others.

The towering hulk of a man standing guard at the warehouse entrance looked him over with eyes that gave the impression that they missed nothing. They would have easily made his blood run cold had he actually been who he claimed to be and not a carefully trained Philadelphia detective, Tate thought, approaching the man.

"Ted Conrad," he said, identifying himself as he held up the driver's license the tech department had crafted for him at the beginning of this operation. Closing the wallet, he slipped it back into his pocket. "I'm on the list."

"Indeed you are, Mr. Conrad, indeed you are."

The voice behind him belonged to the man he'd spoken to on the phone yesterday. As he turned to look at Seth Maddox for the first time, Tate felt the man's arm come around his shoulder as if he and Maddox were old friends.

Even if Randall hadn't found the voice pattern match, recognition would have been immediate once he caught a glimpse of him. It was a familiar face that habitually graced the covers of business magazines and routinely appeared on the pages of the country's business sections. Fortunes were made or lost according to the words Seth Maddox uttered.

"Mr. Seth Maddox, I presume," Tate said dryly.

Maddox eyed him for a moment before the insincere grin bloomed forth. "Right the first time." Playing the grand master and loving the role, Maddox gestured about the huge, festively decorated warehouse as they entered. "Welcome to paradise, Mr. Conrad," he declared with no small fanfare.

Tate was surprised the man didn't have a five-piece orchestra shadowing his footsteps. The place would have warranted it, he couldn't help thinking. Tate took a moment to get his bearings and try to take as much in as he could. He'd seen amusement parks that had less going on.

The warehouse that once housed innocent dolls, stuffed animals, wooden puzzles and train sets was effusively decorated to mimic an artist's conception of Shangri-La.

It looked like an old Arabian Nights movie he'd once seen as a child, Tate couldn't help thinking. Except everything had been supersized. He wasn't very big on fantasy, favoring the truth instead, but it was plain that truth had no place here.

Strategically placed fans were causing filmy pastel-colored drapes to billow out seductively. It did the same for the scanty apparel that Hannah and her friends were forced to wear, emulating harem girls whose only option was to obey the will of their masters.

The way the curtains were positioned along the far wall toward the rear, Tate had a feeling that was where the makeshift "rooms" were located. Rooms where each "buyer" got to "play" with his "merchandise" for the night.

That was where, he thought darkly, the young women, purchased for the night, were taken to be used and abused, feeding lusts of men who would never be satisfied.

"Must have cost a pretty penny to have the warehouse decorated like this," Tate commented, pretending to be impressed as he scanned the surroundings.

"Don't worry, I plan to recoup every penny," Maddox told him with an amused laugh.

"That's your right," Tate agreed. He didn't see Hannah. He could feel his uneasiness grow. Was that his intuition or just his fear of things going wrong? "Not to seem rude, but I'd like to see Jade now," Tate told the man.

He wasn't going to have any peace until he finally got Hannah out of here in one piece and back to her family. But the first step was to locate her. Once he was certain she was all right and all the players were in place, he was going to give the signal for SWAT to come bursting in and finally put an end to this.

"Of course, of course," Maddox was saying in that same mocking voice he'd used on the phone yesterday. "She's right here, Mr. Conrad." Turning, he called to someone in the milling crowd. Because of the din, Tate missed the name.

The next moment, Tate saw a humorless, tall, wiry man bringing in a young woman.

Hannah.

She looked like every man's dream come to life, he thought.

Dressed in swirling layers of see-through, colorful nylon, Hannah looked clearly humiliated. Tate would have given anything to throw his jacket over her to lessen her shame a little. But a gesture like that would be a dead giveaway. It would have been clear that he wasn't here to try to satisfy any perverse appetite.

He needed the charade to continue a little longer. Somehow, he was going to make it up to Hannah, he silently swore.

Hannah's eyes were again filled with wariness as she regarded him.

He was back to square one with her, Tate thought, frustrated. So be it. He resigned himself to that, focusing on his goal for now. It was going to be over soon, he promised himself, slanting a quick glance toward Hannah. He offered her a quick, encouraging smile.

The next moment, a high-pitched noise had him wincing as it proved to be almost unbearable for him.

Maddox looked at him with pity that wouldn't have fooled a five-year-old. "My apologies, Mr. Conrad. Please, come with me."

The next wave of noise was even more jarring.

At the same time, he also noticed that Maddox had managed to herd both him *and* Hannah into a space well removed from the rest of the crowd.

"What *is* that noise?" he demanded as the decibel level increased, practically vibrating inside his ear. It was all he could do not to wince again.

"Why, it's jamming, Mr. Conrad," Maddox told him almost gleefully. The investment guru nodded condescendingly toward his pocket. "Your cell phone won't work here. There's no signal. Sorry, precautions, you understand," Maddox said, watching Tate take in his every word.

Tate was getting a really bad feeling right about now, even as he nodded, playing along. "Makes sense," he acknowledged, inwardly cursing the man.

He was completely cut off from his backup outside, unable to transmit *or* receive instructions. By now Emma and the others had to realize they'd lost the signal. Were they scrambling for another vantage point so that they could renew the connection? Or was he going to have to be the Lone Ranger in this operation after all?

"I'm so glad you agree, Mr. Conrad. Or should I say Detective Colton?" Maddox's smile was malevolent as his eyes bored into Tate. The game was over. "Which do you prefer? And please don't insult me by saying you don't know what I'm talking about. That's so very trite and beneath you, Detective Colton. Besides," he continued as he gestured for his surprise to be brought in, "Mr. Miller already gave you up. He really isn't very much for pain, are you, Solomon?" he asked, his eyes narrowing as he watched the beaten, semiconscious Solomon Miller being brought in, supported by two of Maddox's nameless henchmen.

They were going to kill him, Tate thought. More importantly, they were going to kill Hannah. Maddox would have terminated his own mother without blinking an eye if his agenda called for it. There was no two ways about it. Maddox was an out-and-out sociopath.

Tate knew he had only seconds to do something—or die. He had no weapon, no backup and, at this point, absolutely nothing to lose. Pushing Hannah directly behind him, he grabbed Maddox and bodily shoved him into the incoherent, babbling Miller.

The gun Maddox was brandishing went off.

A scream mingled with a flood of curses. Chaos broke out all at once.

"Go, go, go!" Tate ordered Hannah, grabbing her hand and breaking into a run that took them through the maze of filmy curtains, wisps of smoke and mingling bodies.

Tate had no idea where he was going, all he knew was that they had to get out of here if they wanted to live out the night.

Chapter 6

There was nothing but static coming through.

The eerie sound filled the interior of the van where Emma, Randall and another Bureau tech were currently sequestered, monitoring the transmissions and waiting for Tate to give the signal to initiate the takedown.

The SWAT team was aching to rush the warehouse. The last time she'd checked, their eagerness was puncturing the very air.

"Tate," Emma cried, urgency rising in her voice. "Tate, can you hear me?"

Nothing but more static answered her.

They'd lost him.

Emma felt an iciness spread out through her limbs as her heart all but froze in her chest. She struggled to keep her fear at bay.

This isn't happening.

"Try a different frequency," she ordered Randall,

the tech closest to her. He was already doing just that, as was his partner.

Tate would get out of this, she told herself. He was a survivor.

The static continued as if to mock their efforts.

"Nothing," Randall lamented, exasperated, his eyes focused on the monitor he was trying in vain to adjust. "They're jamming us," he declared in frustration.

Which meant someone was onto them, Emma thought. Someone had told Maddox.

It was all falling apart. Something was very, very wrong.

The door to the van opened and Abe Kormann, the head of the SWAT team, stuck his head in. One look at the faces of the van's inhabitants and he knew something was awry. No one had ordered them in yet and by his reckoning, it was past time.

He looked at Emma. "What do you want to do?" he asked.

She weighed the options. They could wait, and her brother could lose his life, if he hadn't already. Or the SWAT team could rush the warehouse and Tate could get killed in the cross fire. Either option wasn't very good, but she knew that Tate believed the same way she did: that to go down fighting was a far better way to go than to meekly accept defeat.

"Go in," she ordered, then repeated the command, her voice stronger and more confident the second time. "Go in!"

Weapons raised and at the ready, the men and women comprising the SWAT team quickly flew across the expanse that was between the van and the entrance to the warehouse.

They closed the distance in less than five seconds.

The hulking three-hundred-pound-plus bouncer guarding the door reacted automatically, producing a gun. He never got the opportunity to discharge it. The barrel was still pointed down when a marksman's bullet hit him. The bouncer dropped like a stone.

Several men on the team used a ram to break down the warehouse door. It splintered and fell to the ground, useless, as the SWAT team quickly infiltrated the former warehouse.

Screams and cries of confusion greeted their appearance.

People began running in all directions, bumping into one another, adding to the mass chaos.

More screams, gunfire and monumental panic broke out moments after the first shot inside the warehouse was fired. Having the building stormed by men and women in full black regalia with guns drawn only added to the sense of disorientation and imminent danger.

It was a classic case of every man and woman for themselves.

"What's happening?" Hannah cried as she ran alongside Tate, stretching her legs as far as she could as she desperately tried to keep up with the man who was holding on to her hand.

They'd given her drugs shortly before the event had started, but she'd managed to fool them again, pretending to swallow the pills only to hide them between her upper lip and gum. Less had dissolved this time, so she was not as affected as she had been the first time. She was aware of everything.

"You're being rescued," Tate shouted to her so she could hear him above the almost-deafening noise and gunfire.

It was only a half truth at best. The sting had obviously gone awry. But those were still his people who'd burst in, firing their weapons. If there was any justice in the world, Maddox would be captured—if he wasn't already.

But life had taught Tate not to make any assumptions—logical or emotional—until he could verify them with his own eyes.

For now, he and Hannah had to keep going. He didn't want her to stop, not even for a moment. They needed to put as much distance between them and Maddox and his people as possible before he could even remotely entertain the possibility that Hannah was safe. Only then would he stop to find out if Maddox was among the captured or, better yet, among the casualties.

At this point, he really didn't care which it was, as long as the operation could be put to an end and the girls returned to their families.

Abruptly, their path was suddenly blocked by one of Maddox's tuxedoed henchmen. Equal parts fearful and angry, the man clutched a rapid-fire weapon in his hands. Raising it quickly, he didn't warn them to stop, he just began discharging the weapon.

Tate pushed Hannah to the ground as he simultaneously lowered his head and charged into the gunman. Catching the man completely off guard, Tate knocked him down. Moving quickly, Tate had the man's gun before the criminal could recover it.

The weapon discharged once.

The henchman stopped moving.

Tate stood back up, exhaling slowly. Behind him, he heard Hannah's sharp gasp.

"He's dead," she cried in horrified wonder. It didn't seem real to her.

"He was the minute Maddox recruited him," Tate informed her crisply, his voice devoid of any feeling. He held on to the dead man's weapon. They might still need it.

Pulling Hannah to her feet, his eyes swept over her quickly, making assessments. "Are you hurt?" he asked as gently as possible.

Hannah shook her head. "No, I'm not hurt." Her eyes were wide, like someone trapped in the middle of a nightmare that wouldn't end.

"Then let's go," he ordered, taking her hand and running again.

He'd looked up a schematic of the warehouse on an official website listing building plans filed with the city. He liked knowing where he was going before he began his journey.

"I think there's a side exit we can use," he told her.

Tate was relying on what his mother had once referred to as his uncanny sense of direction, picking his way through the maze of interwoven bodies and mayhem. Getting to the exit felt as if it was taking forever, but finally, he could make it out in the distance. The end of the rainbow.

The end of the rainbow in this case was a door to the outside world. Freedom was just beyond that.

Hannah was breathing audibly by the time they finally reached the door. He looked at her over his shoulder again to assure himself that she was all right. "Hang in there." He flashed her an encouraging smile.

Unable to answer, Hannah nodded vigorously instead, offering a hint of a smile. It was all she could muster for now.

Hannah was accustomed to running. Running games among the children had been common when she was growing up, and she had always been one of the faster ones. But the stakes had never been this high and the course had never been littered with bodies before. It made a huge difference.

As they approached the exit, Tate offered up a quick one-line prayer of thanksgiving.

The door wouldn't budge.

Swallowing the curse that automatically rose to his lips in deference to the woman with him, Tate put his shoulder to the door and slammed it hard. The movement was almost imperceptible.

He tried again.

The third time, the door shuddered, then finally moved. One more full-on attack and the door abruptly gave way completely. He was still holding on to Hannah's hand and they both all but fell onto the ground on the other side.

"Success," Tate cried, relieved.

Relief dissipated immediately in the face of the frigid weather. The temperature had dropped even further and there was snow falling, sticking to the ground. Its pristine appearance provided a complete contrast to the angry red smear on the ground not two feet away from where they'd almost fallen.

Someone had escaped ahead of them. And then been killed.

Tate dropped to the ground, pulling her with him as he quickly scanned the immediate area, looking for a sniper. But whoever had killed the man on the ground was no longer there.

Taking a tentative breath, Tate cautiously rose back to his feet, momentarily blocking out the wall of noise echoing from the building behind him.

That was when he realized that Hannah was shaking.

Not from any overt display of fear—not that he would have blamed her if she had been—but from the cold. The thermometer was undoubtedly registering in the low thirties and the outfit her captors had forced her to wear was one far better suited to tropical weather.

Tate shrugged out of his jacket and quickly draped it around Hannah's shoulders, pulling it closed around her. It covered more than half her body.

"It's not much," he apologized. "But at least it's warmer than what you've got on."

Clutching the two sides of the jacket to her to trap whatever heat she could, Hannah nodded her head in thanks. "This helps a lot, thank you. But what about you?"

They were in the middle of what felt like an apocalypse and the woman was being polite. Tate could only shake his head in admiration and wonder. Hannah Troyer was one very special woman, even without taking her beauty into account. The combination was almost more than one man could bear. "I'll be fine," he assured her.

The sound of running feet approaching had Tate pushing her behind him. Hannah's back was protected by the wall while he was shielding the front of her with his body. The next moment, catching a glimmer of what turned out to be moonlight on the barrel of a gun, Tate reacted at lightning speed and fired.

An assailant transformed into a casualty, dropping to his knees and attempting to fire one last time. But the weapon slipped from his lifeless fingers before he could discharge it.

Tate heard Hannah stifle a scream.

"I know him," she cried. He turned to look at her as

she explained, "He was the one who took us, who took Mary and me prisoner and brought us to that motel."

"He won't be taking anyone anywhere anymore," Tate assured her grimly.

They needed to keep going. He couldn't afford to hang around here, waiting for the dust to settle and a body count to begin. His cover had been blown and Maddox's people knew he was a detective. If any of them got away, that made his life worth less than nothing and his death immensely desirable.

As for Hannah, she would simply be collateral damage if they killed him. He needed to get her somewhere safe—and fast. He could gather information later, once he knew she was safe. Or as safe as possible, given that she was a material witness that the state undoubtedly would want to build their whole case on.

He quickly scanned the area, looking for a means of escape. His eyes came to rest on their way out.

"My car," he declared, thinking out loud. When Hannah looked at him quizzically, he pointed to the Ferrari at the far end of the parking lot. The team had secured the vehicle to flesh out the persona he was playing in this sting-gone-wrong. "Over there."

He didn't have to add the word *run*. Hannah was already doing that.

Reaching the vehicle, he yanked open the unlocked door and pushed Hannah inside, then slid across the hood rather than rounding the short distance to the driver's side.

He got in, then threw the car into gear. Less than a second later, he was tearing out of the lot, as if the very forces of hell were right behind him.

Because they very well might have been. He wasn't sticking around to find out.

* * *

He didn't know where else to go.

With a shameful lack of contingency plans, Tate had no choice but to drive to the small apartment he maintained in the heart of Philly. He went there rather than to the hotel room he'd been staying in under his assumed name. The latter would have been the first place he knew Maddox or his men would look, provided they'd eluded capture.

He was still hoping that they hadn't.

The apartment was just a temporary stopover, he told himself. He'd regroup and get in contact with his team so he could get filled in on exactly what the hell had gone down. Equally as important, he had to stop by the place to get his backup weapon. He felt naked unless he was packing both his weapons and doubly so since he'd been forced to leave them both behind to carry off this now-failed charade.

What had tipped Maddox off? Had he been suspicious all along or had Miller slipped up and said something that had clued the man in?

He needed to get answers.

But first, he needed to get his weapons, he reminded himself. The one he'd taken off the dead man had served him well enough, but he wanted a familiar piece in his hands if he was going to have to defend Hannah, as well as himself, for who knew how long. He knew both his piece and his backup piece inside and out, knew they wouldn't fail him or jam. He took better care of the weapons than some men took care of their wives.

Because his life depended on them.

As he drove the Ferrari into the underground parking structure beneath his apartment building, Tate could feel Hannah stiffening beside him. "What's wrong?" he asked her.

"What is this place?" she asked, tilting her head slightly so that she could get a better view of the immediate area.

Tate brought the expensive vehicle to a stop in the parking spot assigned to his apartment number. Ordinarily, his vintage Mustang occupied the space. But right now, it was in the shop for its hundred-thousand-mile tune-up, leaving his parking space conveniently empty.

"This place is where I live," he told Hannah, answering her question. "My apartment's up on the third floor."

Despite recent events, she still wasn't accustomed to buildings rising above a second level. They made her nervous, as if she was waiting for the floors to buckle under the accumulated weight.

"Your family won't mind your bringing me?" she asked him uneasily.

Looking carefully around, just in case, he saw nothing suspicious or out of the ordinary. Only then did he reach in and, taking her hand, help Hannah out of the car. He remained alert as he guided her to the elevator. "My family's scattered," he told her.

The elevator arrived and they got in. He took one last look before the doors closed to make sure no one was suddenly approaching them.

Then he turned his attention to Hannah.

He knew all there was to know about her, he thought, but she didn't know the first thing about him. Maybe she'd feel a little more at ease if he clarified a few minor points for her.

"I'm not married," he told her as they rode up.

"Oh."

She pressed her lips together, feeling oddly happy over the information she was digesting. Was that wrong? In the middle of all this discord and death, she found herself relishing the knowledge that the man who had come back for her, who had rescued her, just as he'd promised, was unattached.

It gave her definite reason to smile.

Shouldn't she be feeling guilty about that instead of strangely jubilant?

When the elevator doors parted, Hannah began to step out of the car only to have him put his hand up before her, stopping her in her tracks. Keeping her in place, Tate moved ahead and looked to the left and right of the elevator, the way a child might if he were crossing the street without an adult accompanying him.

"Okay," he told her, beckoning her off the elevator car.

Tate led the way down the hall to his apartment door. Unlocking it, he went in first, making sure that she was half a step behind him.

The gun he had secured earlier was still in his hand as he scanned the remarkably neat one-bedroom apartment, looking for a telltale shadow, or something to tell him that he and Hannah were not alone in the apartment.

But they were.

He let his guard down just the slightest bit.

Meanwhile, Hannah was taking a survey of her own. "You keep a very tidy home," she told him.

He didn't tell her that he kept it that way because that made it easier to see if something had been disturbed. It was how he could tell if his living quarters had been compromised or not.

The same precautions applied to his dresser drawers. The contents of the drawers were arranged so that he could place an old volume of Shakespeare's sonnets in them without having the book touch anything else in the drawer. If it did touch something else, that meant that someone had been going through his things and had put everything back carefully—but not carefully enough.

Rather than go into any of this, Tate simply replied, "The nanny was strict."

Hannah looked at him, her interest piqued about this outsider more than she knew her brother and the others would think seemly. Secretly, she didn't care.

"You had a nanny?" she asked Tate in wonder. "Where was your mother?" She couldn't imagine one of the women in her village entrusting someone else to look after her children for anything more than a few hours. Certainly not on an ongoing basis.

"She was helping my father build a proud foundation," he answered.

Since the rooms were clear, he went about his final test—checking the volume of sonnets in the drawer—and found everything where it was supposed to be. Finally relaxing, he turned to look at the young woman he'd just brought into his world.

It occurred to him that Hannah and he could not have been more different. Her world was one of simplicity, of tranquillity and almost monasticlike dedication, while his was infused with danger and criminals, never mind the underlying social complexities he and his siblings had grown up with.

They were as different as night and day. And had just as much of a chance of coming together on any level as the sun had of swallowing up the moon.

Even so, he could finally understand what the French meant by their age-old expression, *Vive la différence*.

An image of the country mouse and the city mouse— a story one of the nannies had told him eons ago—suddenly flashed through his mind.

He'd never once thought that the country mouse could be so compellingly attractive.

Learned something new every day, he thought to himself with a broad smile.

Chapter 7

Tate flipped the three locks on his fireproof door one at a time, securing his apartment—at least for the time being.

Even so, he was aware that, as far as time went, they didn't have much of it.

Still, there was enough available to address a few basic amenities.

"Are you hungry?" he asked Hannah.

She shook her head, her long wavy red hair gently echoing the movement a fraction of a second afterwards.

"No. I am a little cold, however," she ventured shyly, as if she felt it was thoughtless and self-centered of her to complain about anything after Tate had risked his life to save hers.

"Right." And why shouldn't she be cold, he realized. The jacket he'd given her was more like a pup tent, but underneath it Hannah was only wearing what amounted to colored scarves in the dead of winter. "Follow me. Let's see what I can come up with," he told her, leading the way into his bedroom at the rear of the apartment.

Opening his closet, he paused and shook his head. There wasn't exactly much to work with. He was a good nine inches taller than she was, as well as wider. Anything of his would fit Hannah at least twice over, if not more so.

"I'm afraid I don't have anything in your size," he apologized. Feeling out of his element, Tate stepped back from his closet and gestured toward it. "Why don't you see if there's anything you can do with what you find?" He saw the uncertain look on her face, as if she didn't feel right about touching anything. The young woman was really amazingly polite, given the circumstances.

"No, I couldn't," she demurred.

They were going to have to leave soon and he knew they wouldn't get very far with her all but immobilized from the cold.

"Yes, you could," he told her firmly, adding, "Feel free to take anything you find," he urged. "I insist." He jerked his thumb back toward the front of the apartment. "I'm just going to be out in the living room, calling my team to find out if anyone knows what happened."

With that, Tate left her to make her choices in peace.

Damn, for a man who was always in control of the situation, Hannah made him feel as if he was tripping over his own tongue. So much for being a savvy police detective, he thought cryptically.

But then, he couldn't remember ever coming across anyone like Hannah Troyer before, he thought. For all intents and purposes, the young Amish woman represented another world to him. A less complicated, more honest world.

There were times, such as now, when he had to wonder if progress, which had gotten them so far away from that simple world, was ultimately worth it, despite all the perks it had to offer.

Maybe Emma had the right idea after all, turning her back on this fast-paced world.

That wasn't his to debate, Tate reminded himself. He didn't have the time. What *was* his to do, he thought, was to check in with his team and find out what the hell was going on—and just where they were supposed to go from here.

He swallowed an oath when his call didn't go through the first time. The signal was too weak. Trying again, he was rewarded with an icon that declared his signal bars were stronger.

The second he said "Hello," he thought his eardrum was going to be shattered.

"Tate?" Emma cried, shouting his name into the phone, a mix of joy and anger evident in the single utterance. "Where the hell are you?" she demanded, then, before he could say a word, she breathlessly demanded, "Do you have Hannah with you?"

Tate was glad he could give his sister *some* sort of positive news.

"Yes, she's here," he acknowledged. "Safe with me for the time being. Your turn," he declared, indicating that it was her turn to answer a question. "What happened with the sting?"

"I was going to ask you the same thing," Emma countered. "Why didn't you give the signal for the SWAT team to storm the warehouse?"

She didn't know. He would have thought that Miller

would have filled her in—unless he couldn't, Tate suddenly realized. Had Maddox killed him?

"I didn't get a chance," he admitted. "Miller blew my cover."

"What?"

He could almost envision the surprise on Emma's face. She and Caleb had been the ones to trust Miller in the first place, and urged the members of the task force to do the same.

"I don't know how, but Maddox got wind of the fact that I was a cop. I think he planned on shooting both of us." He realized how vague that must have sounded to Emma and was quick to clarify the ambiguity. "Hannah and me."

"So you shot him?"

There was no missing the hopeful note in his sister's voice. Was that because she was asking him if he was the one who killed Maddox or did she just hope that the organization's kingpin had been taken down even though he was still among the missing?

"No weapon, remember?" he reminded his sister. "I shoved Maddox into one of his henchmen and his gun went off. After that, I don't know what went down," he admitted. "Did you get Maddox?" The pause on the other end of the line turned into a lengthy silence and it wasn't because he'd lost the signal again. The bars were dark and plentiful.

Tate had his answer.

Damn!

Still, he asked, on the minuscule chance that he was wrong. "You didn't, did you?"

"No." It cost her to admit that. Emma didn't tolerate failure well, especially not her own. "From what I can gather, Maddox and a couple of his guys managed to get away." She paused a moment and Tate knew what was coming. She was trying to find a way to tell him.

They'd both found that straightforward had always been the best way.

"He'll come looking for her," she warned.

Tate knew Emma was talking about Hannah. After all, from what they were learning about the operation, it was quite possible that Hannah had been privy to everything that had happened. He had a feeling that it would only take the memory of her dead girlfriends to get her to testify against the kidnappers.

That fact made her an immense liability for Maddox and it placed her life in immediate danger.

From now on, until they caught Maddox or eliminated him, his only assignment was to keep Hannah safe. Nothing else mattered.

"Yeah, I know."

He paused for a moment, thinking. He could hear his closet door moving along the runners in the bedroom. Hannah was trying to find something to wear and most likely discovering that he had nothing she could use. But desperate times called for adjustments and so far, Hannah had been a trouper. He hoped that she would continue to be one awhile longer.

"I'm going to have to take off for a while until you and the team can find Maddox and bring him down," he finally said to his sister.

He heard Emma laugh shortly. "Tell me something I don't know."

There was a noise behind him and Tate instantly whirled around on his heel, the weapon in his hand raised and ready to fire.

He lowered it when he saw Hannah's terrified expression.

"Sorry," he apologized, then said to his sister, "Hold on for a minute, Em."

Hannah really looked like a teenager now, he couldn't help thinking as he looked at her. She was wearing one of the old blue T-shirts he used to knock around in. She'd gathered it at her waist and tied it tightly so that it didn't look as if she was wearing a potato sack. She also had on a pair of his old, worn jeans rolled up at the cuffs and securely tied at the waist with a scarf just beneath the T-shirt.

He guessed that she must have found the jeans lying discarded somewhere in the back of his closet. He'd been meaning to donate those things to the local charity. Good thing he hadn't gotten around to it.

Just looking at her made him ache.

Rousing himself, he nodded his acknowledgment of her ensemble. "Not bad."

The smile on Hannah's face was sweet as well as shy. "You're being kind," she told him. "I hope you don't mind my wearing these things. I promise to wash them when I'm done."

He shook his head. "Wasn't really worried about that," he assured her.

For someone who'd been abducted and had encountered more evil in the past couple months than she'd ever dreamed existed in the world, Hannah seemed to be holding up remarkably well, he thought.

He suddenly remembered something Hannah had said to him regarding her brother. She'd asked if he'd seen Caleb and if her brother was well. The single question encapsulated the sort of person she was: not a thought about herself, only about others.

Mumbling "Excuse me for a second," Tate turned

his back to her and took his hand off the cell phone's mouthpiece. "Emma?"

"Still here, Tate," he heard his sister answer patiently.

"Is Caleb with you?"

Officially, the man wasn't supposed to be anywhere near the now-failed sting, but knowing Emma and her soft heart, she'd probably not only allowed Caleb to come along, but was probably even now reassuring the man that his sister had been rescued.

"Yes, why?" Emma asked, lowering her voice.

Tate slanted a look toward Hannah before continuing. "I thought he might want to say a few words to his sister," Tate answered. "I know she'd really like to hear from him."

"Hold on a second," Emma responded. He could hear the excitement in her voice. It told him all he needed to know about her relationship with Caleb. Though she wouldn't say it, he now realized that Emma was simply crazy about the man.

Listening, Tate heard some kind of noise in the background, as if she was walking somewhere. And then he heard Emma calling to Hannah's brother. For his part, Tate caught Hannah's eye and beckoned the young woman over to him.

Hannah approached, her beautiful eyes filled with curiosity. Without a doubt, he could very easily spend the next hundred hours or so wading in those mesmerizing blue-gray pools.

The next moment, he upbraided himself for letting his thoughts stray so drastically from the path he needed to follow. He was supposed to be protecting Hannah, keeping her out of harm's way, not drooling over her like some lovesick pubescent idiot.

"Yes?" Hannah asked when he didn't say anything enlightening to her.

"I think there's someone on the other end of this phone who'd like to talk to you," Tate told her.

He offered her his cell phone. She took it from him uncertainly, holding the small item as if it was alive and could leap from her fingers at any moment. That was when he remembered that Hannah probably didn't have the vaguest idea what to do with a cell phone. Or a landline for that matter.

Given her lifestyle, she would have had no reason to have any experience with either one.

"You listen on this part," he told her, pointing out the cell phone's upper portion. "And talk into this." He indicated the tiny holes on the bottom of the cell.

Very gently, he placed the cell phone against her ear. She covered his hand with her own and for a second, he left it right where it was, savoring the contact and absolving himself because he hadn't initiated it.

After a moment, he slipped his hand away and let Hannah hold the phone herself.

"Hannah?"

Her face lit up like a Christmas tree as she recognized her brother's voice coming out of the strange device.

"Caleb! Oh, it's so good to hear your voice!" she cried enthusiastically. The next moment, she fell silent, earnestly listening to what her brother was saying. Tate saw her smile. "No, no, I'm fine. Really. Tate is taking good care of me." She turned her eyes toward him and her smile deepened. "He rescued me, just as he said he would. He told me you sent him, Caleb," she went on. "I confess I didn't believe him, but now I see I was wrong to doubt him. I am safe and unharmed."

She was holding the phone with both hands now, as if that could somehow anchor her brother to her. "When can I see you, Caleb?" she wanted to know.

It was time to interrupt, Tate thought, even though he hated to do it because she looked so happy to be reunited with her brother. But the longer they delayed getting out of here, the more of a risk they ran of being discovered.

"Soon," Tate promised her, gently removing the cell phone from her hands. "Very soon." Putting the phone to his ear, he made a request of the man on the other end. "Caleb, I need to have a word with my sister."

"One moment" was the restrained, polite reply. Tate heard the phone changing hands. Within seconds, he found himself on the phone with Emma again.

Before he could say anything, he heard her telling him, "That was a very nice thing you just did." Since Emma wasn't in the habit of giving compliments, Tate took her words to heart. "It meant the world to Caleb to get a chance to talk to Hannah instead of just having me reassure him that his sister was all right."

"I'm a very nice kind of guy, remember?" Tate countered wryly. "Look, we've got to get ready to take off," he said abruptly. "I'll be in touch when I figure out where we've landed." That was a lie, because he'd already figured that out. He'd just said that in case his line was being tapped or his apartment was being bugged.

He left the rest unsaid, but he didn't have to elaborate. They both knew that the less said, the less chance he ran of their being caught. Right now, Hannah's safety was paramount to him, not just because the entire case against Maddox could very well rest on her slender shoulders if the other girls wouldn't come forward as witnesses, but because he just couldn't bear the thought of any harm coming to her.

Ever.

"You be careful," Emma cautioned.

He heard the concern in her voice, heard the catch in her throat that told him she was trying hard not to let her emotions get the better of her.

It wasn't an easy life either one of them had chosen. The only difference was, Emma would be out of it soon. As for him, he usually thrived on this sort of thing. It was just every now and then that he caught himself wondering what it might be like to have a regular life like the people he saw going about their business every day.

There were times he couldn't help envying some of them. But the truth of it was, he loved what he did and wouldn't have left that world for anything.

"Always," he said belatedly, responding to Emma's order that he remain safe. With that, he ended the call.

He was using one of those disposable phones and at this point, it had served its purpose. He tossed it on the ground and deliberately stepped on it, destroying all chance of the phone's signal being traced.

The young woman beside him gasped and looked at him, a wariness entering her eyes.

She probably thought she'd witnessed a fit of temper, he guessed.

"We don't want to risk being followed," Tate told her. "And that phone would have given off a traceable signal."

"Like a telegraph?" she guessed, trying to relate what he'd just said to her to something she was remotely familiar with.

Tate did his best not to grin as he nodded. "Something like that," he said, even though what he'd actually been thinking of was a GPS.

Hurrying into the bedroom, he pulled a backpack out of the closet and quickly threw some basic items of clothing into it. Then he picked up a winter jacket and held it out to Hannah. "This might fit you a little better than my jacket did," he told her. The jacket was by no means small, but it had fit him when he was less muscular than he was now, since weight training had become a central focus in his life. It was definitely smaller than the jacket he'd draped over her shoulders earlier and she was going to need something substantial to help shield her from the cold.

Hannah took the down jacket from him and slipped it on. As expected, her hands disappeared beneath the sleeves. A quick glance in her direction would have pegged her—mistakenly—as a waif instead of the brave young woman she actually was. Hannah seemed to take all that life threw at her in stride and with a smile.

"We are leaving?" she asked him.

He nodded. "We have to. They're going to be looking for us."

She didn't ask him who *they* were. She knew. She also knew something else.

"For me," Hannah corrected.

That sounded much too isolated. She wasn't a lone wolf and, for the duration, neither was he.

"Since I'll be with you every step of the way, it's really *us,* not you," he pointed out.

For once, she dug in, maintaining her position. Having Tate risk his life for her once was hard enough on her. More than that made her feel an obligation she worried she could never be able to repay.

"But you would not be in danger if you didn't go with me," she pointed out.

He shrugged indifferently. "Makes no difference," he told her. "I *am* going with you so there's no point in talking about it."

He didn't expect her to continue trying to get him to change his mind, but he also didn't expect what happened next.

Hannah rose up on her toes and brushed the very lightest of kisses against his cheek.

On his end, it felt as if the wing of a butterfly had lightly grazed his skin.

When he looked at her quizzically, his fingers just barely brushing against his cheek, Hannah smiled at him. The smile crinkled into her vivid eyes. "You are a good man, Tate Colton."

"Just doing my job," he murmured self-consciously.

She nodded, taking that into account. "You are still a good man," she insisted quietly.

Just then, he thought he heard a commotion directly below them coming from the street level. Hurrying to a window, he looked down and saw that a sleek black Mercedes had pulled up in front of his building.

Several men came pouring out, all dressed in dark suits, as if they had come to pay respects to the dead, rather than try to add one more to Death's numbers. Even from his present vantage point, he could see they were intent on getting their job done.

He didn't have to guess what that "job" was.

He recognized one of the men from the warehouse.

Taking the fire escape to elude them was out of the question. The fire escape outside his apartment faced the front of the building and one of the men was left standing guard by the Mercedes.

But he wasn't about to stay here, waiting to be taken down. Ultimately, the fire escape was the only chance they had to get out.

Grabbing Hannah's hand in his as he slung the backpack over his other shoulder, he ordered, "Let's go."

Hannah wordlessly fell into step beside him, ready to follow him to the gates of hell and beyond, if need be, because of all that he had done for her so far. For this very reason, she felt that she owed him her allegiance and her loyalty.

Besides, she knew in her heart that Tate would keep her safe.

Chapter 8

Tate threw open the window leading out onto the fire escape. A quick glance down told him that Maddox's guard was still there. He just hoped that the man wouldn't decide to suddenly look up until they had cleared the area.

"Are we climbing out the window onto *that?*" Hannah asked, her eyes widening at the very thought.

He realized that she'd probably never encountered a fire escape before, certainly never climbed one before. "It'll hold us," he assured her. "We're going to be going up to the roof."

Rather than question him any further, she stoically said, "All right," and followed him out onto the structure.

"You go first," he instructed softly, pointing to the stairs that led up to the roof. If the guard *did* look up, the henchman would see his back first. And if the guard fired, then *he'd* be the one hit, not Hannah. "Nothing to be afraid of," Tate assured her. He tapped the handrailing. "Everything's solid."

Hannah offered him a wan smile as she made her way up the fire escape of the forty-year-old, six-story building. She kept her eyes trained on the next rung and tried not to think about what a long, long way down it was.

Her fear of heights kept her from even climbing into the hayloft in their barn back home, but she couldn't impose her fears on Tate. It wouldn't be right. Besides, he wouldn't be asking her to do this if there was any other way to make their escape. So, with icy hands, Hannah clung to the black metal handrails and made her way up the metal steps of the fire escape, praying she wouldn't fall and embarrass herself—or possibly worse.

An eternity later, her heart pounding in her chest, she finally reached the roof. Her legs numb, she made herself move out of the way so that Tate could climb onto the roof as well.

Taking a deep breath to help steady her throbbing pulse, she looked at the man who had rescued her, utterly confused. "We are going to hide up here?"

He shook his head. "No, with any luck, we're going to go down the back fire escape."

Before Hannah could think to ask him why hadn't they just climbed down to begin with, Tate swiftly crossed the flat, gravel-paved roof. Leaning over the side of the building, he looked down to the ground below. The rear of the building was facing the alley and it was empty.

No witnesses to give them away.

So far, so good, Tate thought.

Turning toward Hannah, he waved her on. "C'mon," he urged. "Follow me."

Hannah did just that, climbing down six flights without uttering a single word, either in protest or in fear.

Even in the midst of a situation that could become explosive at any moment, Tate had to marvel how incredibly trusting Hannah was.

He'd never met anyone quite like her, he caught himself thinking again.

Focus! Tate upbraided himself sharply.

Now wasn't the time to let his mind wander, making peripheral observations about a girl who was way too young for him. And way too pure. She deserved someone who wasn't nearly as jaded as he had become.

What mattered here, he reminded himself, was for him to remain alert in case one of Maddox's men spotted them or unexpectedly showed up. If Tate slipped up and got distracted, even for a second, it would be all over for them.

All over for her.

And all the risks that had been taken would have been for nothing.

Silently indicating that she was to remain behind him, not beside him, Tate stopped dead when he got to the side of the building.

The street was just beyond that—the unprotected street that offered no shelter until they reached the other side.

Tate slowly edged out, his backup piece in his hand, loaded, cocked and ready to fire if he needed to.

The street was clear. And almost eerily empty. Hazy yellow-white light from the towering streetlamps pooled on the ground, crisscrossing and touching in several places.

"Run," he ordered, taking her hand again and leading the way.

They ran for two long city blocks, passing storefronts, pizzerias and shops that had long since closed their doors. Only the bars had glimmers of muted light emerging through their darkly tinted bay windows, but their doors remained firmly closed. Whatever patrons were left inside were far too involved with their personal brand of poison to give either him or the young woman with him even a first thought, much less a second one.

It was there.

A dusty, navy blue—almost black—sedan that wouldn't have caused anyone's head to turn, either in curiosity or admiration, was parked unobtrusively, just a little beyond the crosswalk.

Tate realized after the fact that until he saw the vehicle parked at the curb, he'd been holding his breath. He released it now.

When he was less than ten feet away from the dusty sedan, he pressed down on the key in his pocket—the one he'd grabbed as they vacated his apartment—and it made a minor high-pitched noise.

The next second, the car's locks were all jumping to attention, opening at the same time.

"Get in," Tate ordered gruffly.

They didn't have a second to spare. Just because he didn't see them didn't mean that Maddox's men weren't closing in on them.

Hannah obeyed without question, sliding in on the passenger side and closing the door just as Tate got in behind the steering wheel.

"Whose vehicle is this?" she asked.

Since her kidnapping, she'd lost count of the cars

she'd been forced into. Because they all ran together, she hadn't been able to tell one from another.

Riding in cars was still a relatively new phenomenon for her since, up to this point, she had spent all her life around carriages and the horses that pulled them.

This vehicle seemed to look more used than the others, she thought. That made it appear different to her.

"Mine," he told her as he started up the vehicle. It came to life immediately. He paid a local teenager to keep an eye on it and to make sure that the car was started regularly when he was out of town.

This, he thought in satisfaction, was where foresight—and paranoia—paid off. He kept the car here in reserve for just this sort of an unexpected twist—to make good his escape if need be.

"You have two cars?" Hannah asked in wonder as he tore away from the curb.

Any second, he expected to see Maddox's men descending on them. Or, at the very least, the black Mercedes trying to chase them down. One thing he knew for certain. There was no way he was about to hang around and press his luck.

"It's a backup car," he explained, then realized Hannah probably didn't know what that meant. "I have it parked away from my apartment just in case I can't get to the car I usually keep in the parking structure." He didn't add that the car also had a host of emergency supplies stored in the trunk for different contingencies. There was also enough cash in the trunk to see him through whatever initially had sent him on the run. Cash rather than credit cards because it couldn't be traced.

Hannah looked duly impressed by his abbreviated explanation.

The vehicle continued eating up the road, putting distance between them and his apartment.

"You are very prepared. Like a scouting person," she concluded, pleased with her analogy.

"I think you mean Boy Scout," Tate corrected gently, taking care not to hurt her feelings. He didn't want her to think he was talking down to her.

By her expression, the thought had never even occurred to her. Instead, she looked cheerful as she nodded at the term he'd supplied that had eluded her. "Yes, like a Boy Scout."

Sitting back in her seat, Hannah watched the road as it whizzed by, merging into the darkness and disappearing behind them. It occurred to her that the world outside her village was a very large place. Did anyone get the opportunity to explore all of it?

"Where are we going?" she asked.

He couldn't risk going back to his place, since Maddox obviously knew where he lived. Turning up at some small, out-of-the-way hotel or motel didn't appeal to him. It was too isolated and too easily found.

Their best bet, he decided, was to hide in plain sight and there was no better place for that than Manhattan, the very heart of New York City.

Tate couldn't help wondering how Hannah would react to *that* news. Slanting a glance in her direction, he said simply, "We're going to New York."

"The state?" Hannah asked uncertainly.

"The city," he answered.

Tate waited, but she made no comment on the information. Instead, Hannah grew very quiet. So quiet that it began to make him uneasy. He could feel her tension.

"Something wrong?" he asked.

Hannah merely shook her head in response and continued to say nothing.

Rather than ask what was wrong again, he made the assumption that something *was* wrong and instead began to coax her to share her thoughts with him. He felt responsible for her and if he'd said anything to upset her, he needed to know so that he could make it right again.

"Hannah, you can tell me," he told her earnestly. "You can tell me anything."

Hannah looked down at her short, unadorned, rounded nails without really seeing them. She had no right to bother him with her fears. He was the leader out here in this world of outsiders. It wasn't for her to contest his judgment or challenge his choices.

Still, he was asking her to speak and to ignore his request would have been rude of her.

The tug-of-war in her head went on for only a minute. After it was over, in a very small voice she told him. "People die in New York City."

"People die everywhere, Hannah. Are you talking about someone specifically? Did someone you know die when they came to New York?" he added, hoping to prompt her to tell him the source of her fear.

Before he had gotten involved in the case, his notions about the plain-speaking people of the Amish community were admittedly preconceived and incredibly limited. He had no idea that when Amish children reached their later teens, they were allowed—even encouraged—to leave the village and live among the outsiders for a time. It was a test devised to see if they were truly meant to live out the rest of their lives in the village or if life in a large metropolis was what they really wanted.

Solomon Miller belonged to the latter group and, as Tate had come to know, there was obviously a price to pay for that choice. Being ostracized by the community was the heaviest burden. Miller had been willing to risk Maddox's wrath to get back into the good graces of the community he missed so much.

"I had a friend," Hannah began. "Her name was Eva. Eva went to New York City." Hannah turned to look at him. "She never came back."

"Maybe she liked it better there," he suggested. It was, after all, the logical conclusion.

It might have been logical to him, but not to her. Hannah shook her head. "When her mother and father went to see her, to make sure the choice was hers and not made for her by someone else, they found her dead in her small room. She had a noose around her neck."

That sounded like something Maddox might have been mixed up in. Or, if not him, than someone of his ilk, Tate thought.

"She was murdered?" he asked.

Hannah folded her delicate hands in her lap and stared straight ahead at the inky road. "We were not told. No one spoke her name again."

"Well, they'll speak yours," Tate assured her with feeling. "Because nothing's going to happen to you. I promise," he added, his eyes briefly holding hers. "And I haven't broken a promise to you yet, have I?"

"There has only been one," Hannah reminded him politely.

He grinned, knowing that she was going to say that. Predictability sometimes had a nice feel to it, he thought. Like now.

"Yes, but I kept it, didn't I?"

His answer made her smile at him. She looked back at her hands with approval. Her knuckles no longer white and tense.

"Yes, you did," she agreed. He deserved to receive better treatment at her hands. "I am sorry. I did not mean to be such a pull on you."

"Such a—?" And then the light went on in his head as the right word occurred to him. "You mean *drag,* don't you? You didn't mean to be such a drag," he reiterated, piecing together her real meaning. He laughed as what he'd just said played back in his mind. "You're not a drag, trust me."

"I do," she told him solemnly. "I trust you very much."

And that, he knew, meant a great deal to him. Perhaps even a little too much. After all, he was just protecting her the way a bodyguard might.

Nothing more.

Tate drove all night, arriving in the heart of New York City well past dawn. Specifically, he'd arrived at the Old Vic Hotel. The landmark hotel, remodeled more than a handful of times, stood guard over a section of Central Park. He was partial to it.

A valet popped up the second he pulled up before the hotel. He hurried over to the driver's side, ready to take possession of the vehicle from Tate.

But the latter shook his head. Rolling down the window on his side, he told the eager valet, "I'd rather park it myself, thanks."

The valet's disappointment quickly turned to happiness when Tate slipped the man a tip, even though no service had been rendered.

Parking the sedan himself, Tate knew where to locate the car at a moment's notice. It also enabled him to take a small packet out of the trunk before he secured it again. He tried the trunk a number of times right after that until he was certain that it was locked and no one else could access its contents.

There were a couple of passports in the trunk as well. Just in case…

Hannah watched in silence, curious, as he slid the packet open, then withdrew several crisp hundred-dollar bills and pocketed them.

"For the hotel bill," he told her.

She understood money, but she also knew that people in the world beyond her village used something she had heard referred to as "plastic." They used it for everything.

"You do not have plastic?" she asked.

The question amused him because he'd never thought that she'd be the one to ask that.

"This is simpler," he said, nodding at the cash in his hand.

That was the simple answer. The more specific one was that money couldn't be traced while credit cards— even those obtained under a different identity—could. And once they were traced, they could easily set off alarms.

He needed to buy them as much time as he could— literally.

Getting out of the vehicle, Hannah suddenly became very self-conscious. She looked down at what she was wearing. In the world she resided in, no one went visiting looking like an orphaned urchin. She didn't want to embarrass him.

"Won't someone object to the way I am dressed?"

For a long moment, Tate looked at this young, beautiful, unassuming woman he had stumbled across, then smiled.

"Don't worry. No one taking one look at you is going to object to the way you're dressed," he promised.

Hannah appeared unconvinced. "Are you certain?"

"Very certain," he replied, slipping his arm through hers. "Tell you what, after we get a little food into you, why don't we go shopping?"

"Who is *we?*" she wanted to know, thinking he was referring to a friend of his, or perhaps a lady friend he was involved with. The prospect of his bringing along another female, possibly for her input, oddly disturbed her.

He gestured to her and then himself. "You and me. *We,*" he emphasized. "Why?"

She didn't hear the question, just his definition. "No one else?"

"No one else," he told her solemnly.

Was she asking about her brother? he wondered. It wouldn't be safe, having Caleb come all the way out here. For all they knew, one of Maddox's minions was watching Caleb right now, counting on the fact that the man would be coming to see his sister.

Maddox had already demonstrated that he was desperate to eliminate Hannah. Tate was *not* about to drop breadcrumbs to make it easy for the bastard to carry out his murderous intent.

Guiding Hannah through the revolving door—which she regarded with unabashed wonder and amusement—Tate ushered her with him toward the front desk.

"My wife and I would like a suite overlooking Central Park," he told the neatly dressed man at the reservations desk when he finally reached it.

He was aware that standing beside him, Hannah's mouth had dropped open in complete wonder.

Chapter 9

"But I am not your wife," Hannah protested nervously in a hushed whisper as they walked away from the clerk at the reservations desk. Tate, she noted, had something that looked like a rectangular card in his hand. The clerk had given it to him and she couldn't help wondering why.

"I know," he replied. "But I couldn't very well register as Detective Tate Colton and the young woman he just rescued from a sex trafficking ring, now could I?" he pointed out, then grinned to put her at ease. "For one thing, there wasn't enough space. Besides, the less resemblance we bear to who we really are, the better. It's just to throw them off," Tate assured her as they reached the bank of hotel elevators. He hit the up button. It lit up.

Hannah didn't have to ask who he meant by *them*. She knew. Maddox and his men.

"You really think they will be looking for us?" she asked in an almost inaudible voice.

He didn't *think,* he *knew.* But it wouldn't help put her at ease to belabor that point. "Better to take precautions, just in case," he said, deliberately vague in his answer.

The elevator arrived and he ushered her in, then stepped into the car himself. He pressed "4." The gleaming stainless-steel doors slid shut. He noticed Hannah pressing her hand to her abdomen as they ascended, as if to keep it in place.

She wasn't used to this, he thought. It was, he mused, a little like exposing a flower grown in the shade to strong sunlight. Acclimation was going to take time and patience.

The elevator reached their floor and they got out. "But you believe that they will be looking here?" she pressed again, wanting him to give her an answer one way or another.

"They won't find you," he promised. "That's why I'm not planning on letting you out of my sight." Glancing down at the entry card the reservations clerk had given him, Tate scanned both sides of the corridor, then turned to the right, going in search of room 462.

Reaching the room, he was about to slide the keycard to unlock the door when he sensed that she was staring at him. When he looked at her, he saw her brow furrowed in confusion.

"What's wrong?" he asked.

"The man at the desk didn't give you a key," she pointed out. "How are we going to get in?"

There was precious little to smile about in his job so when the opportunity arose, Tate couldn't resist.

"Magic," he answered without cracking a smile. The

next moment, he followed up his claim by opening the door. He gestured for her to enter.

Hannah crossed the threshold, her eyes all but riveted to the door he had just opened. "You did it," she murmured in awe and wonder. "You opened the door. With that *thing*." She pointed to the keycard.

"Always keep my word," he told her.

The moment she was inside the suite, he quickly closed the door and made sure that all the locks were secured and flipped in place.

He was going to have to rig up something of his own before he felt truly protected, he thought. A rank amateur could most likely breach the hotel safety locks if he wanted to.

He'd tried twice to feed her on the way here and she'd turned down the two offers—he had a feeling that her nerves were far too tangled for her to consume anything without having it make her feel sick to her stomach. "If you're not hungry, I suggest you try to get some sleep." As if to reinforce his suggestion, he crossed over to the queen-size bed and turned down the cover for her.

Hannah made no move toward the bed. Instead, she knotted her fingers together and asked in a quiet voice, "Where are you going to sleep?"

She was concerned that he was going to take advantage of the situation, Tate thought. That perhaps he even saw it as payback for rescuing her. Her opinion of the men outside her village wasn't very high, but then, he had to admit he couldn't blame her, seeing as how she'd been forced to deal with only the dregs of the outside world so far.

"Don't worry about me," he said mildly. "I can sleep anywhere."

And he could. He'd gotten accustomed to grabbing

short catnaps whenever he could while working an assignment. But he had no intention of even doing that tonight. He wanted to remain on his guard—just in case they *had* been followed.

Turning toward Hannah, he motioned her to come forward. "Go ahead," he urged. "Get into bed."

This time, moving stiffly, Hannah did as he told her. Drawing the blanket up to her chin and holding on to it as if it was a protective shield, she watched him as intently as she could with eyes that were struggling to remain alert—and open.

Pulling a chair over to the bed—and making sure he was facing the door—Tate sank down into it.

"I could sit in the chair and you could lie down in the bed," she offered, clearly feeling guilty that he had to spend the night sitting in a chair.

Tate shook his head, staying exactly where he was. "Now what kind of a gentleman would that make me?" he wanted to know. "Hogging the bed and making you spend the night sitting up in a chair?"

He saw her brow furrow again. "Hogging?" she repeated, puzzled. The word didn't make any sense to her in its present context.

"It's just an expression," he explained, trying not to laugh at the face she'd made. "In this case, it means not sharing." He looked at her, waiting. "Anything else you want cleared up?"

She shook her head. There wasn't anything right now, but she knew that there would be again. And most likely soon. Living among the outsiders was almost like learning a new language.

"You outsiders—you do not speak plainly," she told him.

Her voice faded away with the last word. She had

lost her battle against sleep and had slipped into its confines, leaving Tate to contemplate his next move in silence.

He put making plans on hold for a moment and allowed himself to just look at the young woman whose life he'd risked everything in order to save. For everything she'd gone through, Hannah looked amazingly unscarred—not to mention incredibly beautiful.

And growing more so by the moment. Was that even possible?

He shook himself free of the thought and forced his mind back to the situation at hand.

Anyone looking at her would have speculated that the worst thing she had to contend with was selecting which ribbons to tie in her hair.

Amish girls don't wear adornments in their hair, he reminded himself. He and Hannah came from two completely different worlds—and she didn't belong in his.

Be that as it may, he couldn't seem to draw his eyes away.

What would it be like, he wondered, having someone like that to come home to every night? A woman who was warm and welcoming and cared whether or not he was happy? Up until now, he'd never thought of his life as lacking anything. Not having a wife or children was something that worked in his favor, since there was no one to consider but himself. If he was hurt, or in a dangerous situation, he wasn't burdened by guilt, worrying about how his wife and family would carry on if something happened and he was killed. None of that ever came into play or hampered him. It left him free to be a better detective, one who didn't hesitate to do whatever it took to get the job done.

That was who and what he was.

If it ain't broke, don't fix it, he told himself, falling back on the timeless adage. And his life wasn't "broke."

No, it wasn't broken by any means, but what it was, he thought, was empty. Oh, he connected with his siblings on occasion. They might not share DNA, but they shared the same values as well as love for the same pair of adoptive parents. And up until a few days ago, that had been enough.

But it didn't feel like enough anymore, he thought, ruefully, watching Hannah's blanket rise and fall as she breathed.

You're getting philosophical in your old age, Colton. Focus on the assignment, don't get all sensitive about what you think is missing in your life. Thinking that way is liable to get you both killed.

It was sound advice. Now all he had to do, Tate thought, was take it.

He stopped looking at Hannah and fixed his attention on the door instead.

Hannah's eyes flew open with a start.

Heart pounding, she quickly looked around, her eyes delving into every corner, every space, trying to understand what she was seeing and what her brain was telling her was true.

She more than half expected to be back in that awful, awful hotel room, huddled three to a bed and chained to some part of it because her kidnappers were taking no chances that she and the other girls might try to escape somehow.

But when her panic eased and she began to actually grasp what she was seeing, Hannah realized that she was still in the same grand-looking suite Tate had brought her to in the wee hours of the morning, before the sun had had a chance to rise—right after they'd escaped from his apartment.

Was all of this really happening to her?

The moment she thought of Tate, she sat up, every fiber of her body acutely alert even before she managed to focus on him.

She looked at him in surprise. He was just where he'd been when she'd closed her eyes. Sitting in an upholstered chair beside the bed.

Had he spent the entire night—or what had been left of it—sitting in what had to be an uncomfortable position, guarding her? Her own body ached in sympathy just *looking* at him.

Scrambling up to her knees, she moved closer to Tate, peering at his face. His eyes were closed.

When they suddenly opened, she was caught off guard and, losing her balance, tumbled backward onto the bed. "I thought you were asleep."

"I wasn't," he told her. "I was just resting my eyes."

She sat up, swinging her legs over the side of the bed. Hannah scooted over, closer to him in case they had to whisper because someone might be listening. Habits learned during her harrowing imprisonment were hard to break.

"You really spent the night in that chair," she marveled. "Isn't it hard to sleep that way?"

"I wasn't trying to sleep," he answered.

So he'd said when she'd offered to switch places with him, she thought. "You were standing—sitting guard," she recalled, amending her words to fit the situation. "But aren't you tired now?" she wanted to know. Then, before he could answer, she made him an offer. "I could stand guard now if you like, wake you if someone tries to come in," she added.

The sweetly selfless offer made him smile. Did she have any idea how adorable that sounded? Most likely not, he decided.

"Thanks for the offer," he told her, "but I'm fine. I don't need a lot of sleep."

"But you need some," she insisted, determined to pay him back somehow. "Everyone needs some."

"And I got what I needed." There'd been a moment or two during the night when he had caught a few winks. He'd learned how to sleep with one eye open at all times. And how to stretch a few winks into making do. The job had trained him to get by on very little. And, conversely, how to make a little go a long way.

Right now, he had something far more important than sleep to attend to. He was hungry and he had a feeling that so was she. There was finally color in her face, and a tiny bit of sparkle in her eyes. He had no doubt that Hannah had a strong personality and was already working at putting what happened to her earlier—the kidnapping, the brutish behavior—behind her.

"Tell you what," he proposed, "why don't you and I get some breakfast and then go shopping?"

"Shopping?" she echoed. Why would he want to go shopping with her? And exactly what sort of shopping was he referring to? "You mean like buying some food for later?"

"No," he corrected, puzzled why she would even think that. "Like buying clothes—for now," Tate emphasized.

She still wasn't completely clear on what he was saying he wanted. "You wish to purchase clothing for yourself?"

He grinned. He knew half a dozen women, his sisters included, who would have instantly jumped at the chance to go shopping before he could have even finished saying the word. This dewy-faced young woman was certainly in a class by herself.

"No," he corrected patiently, "I 'wish to purchase' clothing for you. Not that the waif look you're currently wearing isn't very appealing in its own way…" His voice trailed off deliberately.

It was meant as a teasing remark rather than a revealing one. But the truth was that despite the fact that his clothes—even the smallest ones he had outgrown—were way too big for her, there was something incredibly stirring and enormously appealing about the way Hannah looked when she put them on.

Tate cleared his throat and forced himself to focus on what he was trying to convey to her. So far, he wasn't having much luck—in either focusing or in making himself clear. "Anyway, I thought you might be more comfortable wearing something that actually fit you and belonged to you."

Hannah flushed. She was already in his debt. This would just increase that debt by heaven only knew how much.

"I don't wish to be any trouble," she told him, demurring the offer. "And I have no money to spend on clothing." The fact of it was, she didn't have a penny to her name.

"Let me worry about the money," he told her, then added firmly, "And it won't be any trouble. Besides," he continued with a whimsical smile, "it might be fun." When he said that, he was thinking of her. As far as he was concerned, just being with her, observing how she took everything in—as if she had crossed the threshold into Wonderland—was definitely fun for him. "The store windows are all decorated for the holidays and the city is at its best this time of year."

He wasn't all that partial to New York City, frankly preferring several other cities to the Big Apple. But he had to admit that when it came to celebrating the holidays, the citizens of Manhattan took second place to no one. Store merchants went all out decorating their windows both in tribute to the holidays and in a not-so-subtle attempt to attract customers to shop in their stores.

"We can even stop to look at the Christmas tree in Rockefeller Center." The suggestion drew a blank look from Hannah and he quickly made his assumptions from that. "You've never seen the Christmas tree at Rockefeller Center, have you?"

Her eyes on his, Hannah slowly moved her head from side to side.

This, Tate thought, promised to be a great deal of fun. "Then you have a real treat in store for you," he told her. "Why don't you freshen up and we'll get started?" When she looked at him blankly for a second time, he nodded toward the opened door that was in the rear of the suite. "The bathroom's right in there," he told her. "There are fresh towels and everything else you might need in there. You can take a shower—or a bath if you prefer," he added, thinking that she might not have showers where she came from. He really should have studied up on the basic elements that comprised her Amish lifestyle, he thought. But then, he hadn't known he was going to have this sort of up-close-and-personal contact with the woman he rescued.

"And you will be where while I am in there, 'freshening up'?" she asked him haltingly, a bit of color creeping up her cheeks.

"Right where I am now," he told her. "Out here.

Waiting." He smiled at her. "You can lock the door from the inside, you know."

The expression of surprise on her face told him that she *didn't* know. And then that expression softened into a smile of gratitude.

Hannah rose to her feet. "I'll hurry," she promised, already striding toward the rear of the suite.

"You can take your time," he called after her. "I'm not going anywhere without you."

Hannah looked over her shoulder and smiled at him. She wouldn't have been able to explain to her brother, or to anyone else for that matter who might ask her why, but Tate's assurance was immensely comforting to her. More than she would have thought it should be.

"I will still hurry," she told him. She had been taught never to take advantage of someone's kindness to her, and there was no reason in the world for her to change her behavior now.

Tate couldn't truthfully say that he didn't allow his mind to wander, or that he tried to restrain it from conjuring up fantasies of Hannah slowly easing her nude, firm young body into the tub filled with warm water and soapy bubbles, as he listened to the sound of running water.

His fantasies increased threefold when he realized that the melodic sound coming from the bathroom was *not* someone singing on the radio.

There *was* no radio in the bathroom and Hannah certainly didn't have one with her. Things like that were forbidden in her simple community. No radios, no TVs. What he was listening to was Hannah, singing softly to herself.

Or maybe she was singing to him.

Heaven knew it certainly felt that way as the melody corkscrewed itself into his belly, causing one hell of an earthquake in his gut.

Her singing just added fuel to the daydream that insisted on blooming in his head, taking over all his thoughts.

If she didn't stop singing soon, he was going to need a cold shower himself.

He closed his eyes, which only made things worse. Because then he could vividly envision Hannah, her sleek, supple body submerged in the suds-filled tub of warm water, each movement making the suds recede a little more...

The very image wreaked havoc on his already twisted gut, not to mention on adjoining parts of his body as well.

His job left no time for extracurricular activity, no time for him to remember that he was still human, still a man with a man's needs. He kept that part of himself tightly under wraps because he'd told himself that gratifying those needs wasn't nearly as important as the assignment he undertook.

But being this close to Hannah, to her innocence, her purity, not to mention her exceedingly appealing face and body, unearthed all those thoughts, feelings and reactions he thought he had kept buried so well. Unleashed them in spades.

He wondered if the department gave out awards for sainthood.

It should, he couldn't help thinking, as the volume of her voice swelled and the sheer beauty of it completely encompassed him.

It really, really should.

Chapter 10

When Hannah came out of the bathroom fifteen minutes later, fully dressed, her skin glowing as she was towel-drying her hair, Tate had already made a few decisions as to what their next move had to be.

He was well aware that he was going to have to be at his most persuasive to convince Hannah to go along with something that, although less than an order, had to be more than just a polite suggestion.

However, at the moment, Hannah embodied such an entrancing picture of innocence, he just had to pause and take it all in. How could someone who appeared to look so simple be so stirring at the same time?

Hannah was quick to pick up on her rescuer's ambiguity. Utterly without vanity, she stopped drying her hair, letting it begin to air-dry instead. Given the thickness of her hair, the process would take a long time.

"Is something wrong?" she wanted to know.

"No—well, maybe." He wasn't accustomed to stumbling over his words. It was almost as if he was unsure of himself and he couldn't remember the last time *that* had happened. As a matter of fact, he couldn't recall a single time—which made what he was experiencing all the more irritatingly puzzling. Finally, he said, "It depends on your point of view."

All he had managed to do was make his explanation more confusing, not less. Hannah flashed a shy smile at him as she shook her head. Then, to his surprise, she placed the blame on her inability to comprehend rather than on his inability to communicate.

"I'm sorry, but I still don't understand."

He'd never had trouble making himself understood or getting his point across before. He had a very organized, practical mind that approached everything in a logical fashion. More than once, he'd been accused of being *born* old. But what was going on here, the way his feelings kept scrambling and retreating, would definitely *not* stand up to any close scrutiny. The young woman whose safety he was assigned to ensure was getting to him. Getting under his skin. Big-time.

Tate took a breath and forced himself to be blunt, rather than tiptoeing around the subject. "I think, in order for you to stay safe while the Bureau and the Philly P.D. try to locate Maddox, you're going to have to change your appearance a little." This was one time he couldn't allow himself to soften the blow. It would ultimately be a disservice to her. "Actually, more than a little," he amended.

She was still wearing his jeans and shirt with the cuffs both rolled up as much as possible. Even so, she was all but literally swimming inside the clothing. Hannah looked down at herself, as if trying to home in on what he was referring to. What she was wearing was legions away from her normal garb.

"I thought I had already changed my appearance— more than a little," she underscored.

Tate laughed. There was no getting away from the fact that she looked like an adorable waif. And that, right now, was working against them, rather than in their favor.

"That'll only attract attention. We need you to blend in, not stand out." Without meaning to, he scrutinized her hair as he spoke. "But still look different than you do now."

The shift was not lost on Hannah. She saw the way he was looking at her hair. Instinctively, her hand went up, covering the length that was draped down over her shoulder. But even as she did it, she sensed that the protective gesture was futile.

"You want to cut my hair." It wasn't a question.

But Tate pretended to take it as such. "Do I want to? No," he told her honestly. "But I'm afraid that I think we should. Maddox can afford to have the best men working for him, that means he's going to have professionals looking for you. Looking for a twenty-year-old young woman with long red hair. The less you look like that, the better your chances are of eluding them until my team finally takes him into custody."

For a moment, she focused on the promise of his words. "Do you really think they will?"

He could hear hope fairly throbbing in Hannah's voice. He was glad he didn't have to lie to her, that he believed in what he had to say to her.

"I do. My team is the best of the best," he assured her.

"Then perhaps I don't have to cut it…" Hannah's

voice trailed off for a moment. But before he could tell her that, although he really regretted it, she was going to have to surrender her hair—better for her hair to be cut than for her to be cut down—Hannah took a deep breath, as if resigning herself to what she was about to say next. "It is only hair. It will grow back." Her words were stoic. "Do what you must."

There was more and he wasn't happy about having to say it, but this, too, was necessary. "Hannah, we need to dye your hair as well."

Her eyes widened. No women in her world would have even *considered* adding color to their hair, much less changing that color.

"Dye my hair?" she asked, uttering the words as if each tasted sour on her tongue.

He nodded. "Redheads stand out. Having your hair cut shorter will change your appearance somewhat, but not enough. Making your hair a different color might very well save your life."

Hannah pressed her lips together, suppressing a very real desire to argue with him, to try to save her hair. But despite her desire to keep her hair just the way it was, something inside her sensed that he was right.

"I understand," she replied quietly, squaring her shoulders the way a soldier facing a firing squad might. "Do whatever you need to," she said, giving him blanket permission.

The first thing he needed to do, Tate thought, was to get a hair-dyeing product. There were a variety of shops on the hotel's ground floor, not to mention a slew of stores outside the hotel, all located in the immediate vicinity. He had his pick of where to shop.

For a second he debated leaving Hannah in the hotel room with a strict warning not to open the door to anyone. After all, it would only take him a few minutes to go and purchase the necessary item. Fifteen minutes from start to finish, most likely. But, like a parent with a child who had yet to cross her first street alone, he felt uneasy about the prospect of leaving Hannah alone right now, even for such a short time.

There was another way.

Getting on the phone, Tate called down to the front desk and asked the clerk to connect him to the nearest drugstore.

"Are you ill, sir?" the clerk asked with polite concern.

"No, nothing like that," Tate said quickly. "It's just that my wife thinks her roots are starting to show and she's insisted that I go buy her some of that hair-coloring product she seems to swear by," Tate explained with the air of a long-suffering husband who'd been this route before.

"Would you happen to know what type and color your lovely wife prefers?" the clerk asked dutifully. The man seemed genuinely surprised—as was Hannah—when Tate rattled off the name brand and the exact color number of the hair dye he was requesting. The clerk recovered in the next beat and told him, "As it happens, I believe the pharmacy around the corner just might stock that. I'm dispatching a bellman to purchase a box of the aforementioned product right now. Once he has it, he'll bring it up to your suite—if that's all right with you, sir."

Tate turned to look at Hannah. She appeared somewhat bemused. The sooner they got this over with, the better. "That'll be perfect with me," he replied, then hung up. Hannah, he saw, was still looking at him strangely. "What?" he asked her.

"You know these things?" she marveled, unabashedly surprised. "Do all men in your world know about hair coloring and such?" she asked, curious.

"The ones who worked in beauty salons to earn spending money while in high school do," he quipped. His parents had been decidedly well-off, but they went out of their way to teach all their children that money was not something to be taken for granted, that it had to be *earned* in order to be enjoyed.

So, to that end, he and all his siblings each had jobs—menial jobs—to teach them what it felt like to work hard to earn a dollar. Though he'd grumbled about it at the time, he had since learned to see the wisdom in that approach and was very grateful that his parents cared enough about him to give him such a solid foundation to fall back on.

"A beauty salon, like the one in Eden Falls?" Hannah repeated, clearly intrigued by the concept of his working around women focused on outer beauty instead of inner beauty.

"Yes, just like it."

"Why would a woman waste so much time on her hair?" Hannah asked. In her world, brushing for a hundred strokes was all the time and consideration a woman's hair was allotted. Who had the time to spend so much of it playing with hair and rendering it into unnatural states?

"Not wasted," he corrected amiably. "Hair is referred to as a woman's crowning glory for a reason." He moved closer to her, then lightly brushed his hand over her hair. Sifting it through his fingers, he was hard-pressed to remember ever touching anything that felt so incredibly soft. "You're lucky, it feels naturally silky. A lot of women would love to have your hair."

She looked down at the lock still resting halfway down her breast. "Soon, I will not have it, either."

Tate felt bad for her. He hated having to do this, but the way he saw it, they really had no choice. "I'm not going to shave your head," he pointed out.

She regarded him with those eyes that delved right to his core, picking up on something that hadn't been clear to her before. "Then you are going to be the one to do this?"

Tate nodded. He'd thought this out as well. "It's better that way. The fewer people we encounter while you still have that long red hair, the better. Unless you'd rather have someone more professional do it," he offered. He could see how allowing him to cut and color her hair might make her uneasy.

Despite his training and his protest that he'd do an incredible job, his teenage sister Piper wouldn't let him near her hair. Emma wouldn't either. If Emma needed her hair cut, she went to the same beautician she'd been going to for years.

Well, if she becomes Amish, that's *going to have to change,* he mused.

"No, I trust you," Hannah was saying. The next moment she stifled an exclamation when someone knocked on their suite door.

Fear immediately entered her eyes as they darted from him to the door.

Instantly alert, his hand hovered over the hilt of the weapon he had tucked into his belt at the back of his trousers. It was all hidden from sight beneath his jacket. Tate crossed to the door.

"Who is it?" he wanted to know.

"The hotel bellman, sir." The tenor voice cracked ever so slightly as he identified himself. Tate judged that the bellman was only recently out of his teens. "I have the hair product that your wife requested."

Tate opened the door a crack, just enough to afford him a view of the hallway.

Satisfied that only the bellman was standing outside his door, Tate opened it a little farther—just enough to trade merchandise for cash.

"Thanks," he told the bellman as he attempted to hand the latter a twenty.

The bellman looked at the denomination a little longingly. "Oh, no, sir. The cost of the hair dye will be on the hotel bill," the bellman replied.

Tate nodded. The bellman wasn't telling him anything he didn't already know. "I know. This is for your trouble."

Now that was a whole different story. The bellman thanked him twice before retreating down the hallway, the twenty clutched in his hand.

Closing the door, Tate turned around to find Hannah quietly observing him. He didn't have long to wait to find out why.

"That was a very nice thing you did, giving him that money." While she was not devoted to tracking her own money—or lack of it—she had a healthy respect for all the good money could do if spent the right way.

"It's called a tip," he explained.

Her brow furrowed as she tried to integrate what he'd just said with what she knew already. It didn't quite fit together.

"Isn't a tip something that is said, like advice about something?" she asked.

She was a treasure, she really was, Tate couldn't help thinking, charmed again by her uncomplicated innocence.

"That's another kind of tip," he said out loud.

Hannah shook her head. This was not the first time she'd discovered that the same word could mean two very different, unrelated things. How did these outsiders keep everything straight?

"You *Englischers* have a very strange language," she pronounced with another shake of her head. "So complicated."

He laughed, thinking of several examples of words that would undoubtedly prove Hannah's assessment to be correct. "I guess it is at that."

It was time to get serious, he thought, opening the package of hair dye that the bellman had brought him. He double-checked the color. It was marked light golden brown, just as he'd requested. That should do the trick, he reasoned.

He flashed an encouraging smile at Hannah and said, "C'mon, let's get this over with."

Dutifully, she bobbed her head up and down. She looked around the suite, undecided where to go. "Where do you want me?"

Home, safe, he silently declared.

"Let's go back into the bathroom," he suggested, nodding toward it.

Hannah walked ahead of him, stoic and resigned, a prisoner making her way slowly to her own execution. As she crossed the tiled threshold, he stopped to drag in a chair. He pulled it as close up to the sink as he could and she sat down stiffly without a word. He noticed that she deliberately avoided looking into the mirror.

Probably afraid I'm going to do a hatchet job, he thought. He knew the shorter hair was going to be a shock to her—not to mention when she saw it once it was dyed—but at least he knew that he wasn't going to make a botched job of it.

He cut her hair first.

Hannah sat very still. She kept her eyes closed as if bracing herself to feel each painful snip of the scissors. He noticed her wincing a couple of times, her eyes still squeezed shut. Had to be the anticipation of pain. Either that or she was wincing from the sound of scissors shortening her hair.

When he was finished, he inspected his handiwork with a critical eye. Her long flowing hair had been converted to an appealing bob, with her hair now framing her face and ending somewhere around the bottom of her chin.

Not bad, even if I do say so myself, he congratulated himself silently. *She might even learn to like it.* Granted, it seemed to erase her Amish identity, but the beautiful woman who'd emerged was definitely an unwitting heartbreaker, he couldn't help feeling.

Rousing himself, Tate donned the pair of rubber gloves that came in the box and mixed together the two components that formed the hair dye. He draped a towel around her neck and shoulders as an afterthought, then proceeded to apply the dye mix in long, even streaks, moving methodically until he'd used up every last drop of the solution in the plastic bottle.

Done, he tossed the emptied bottle as well as the box and the rubber gloves into the bag the bellman had brought. Closing the top of the bag he folded it over twice before throwing the bag into the wastebasket.

Sensing he was finished, Hannah asked, "And now?" She still avoided looking at herself in the mirror because she wasn't certain she was up to dealing with what she saw.

"Now we wait for twenty minutes," he told her. Then, because she'd looked at him sharply, waiting for an explanation as to why they had to wait for that particular length of time, he added, "The color has to set."

Even as he said it, he set a timer on his watch for twenty minutes.

When it went off twenty minutes later, as a series of chimes, he motioned her to the sink. "I've got to wash that out now."

Asking no questions, Hannah dutifully sat down in the chair and ducked her head under the faucet. Tate first rinsed the dye out, then worked the conditioner through her hair before thoroughly rinsing that out as well.

Wielding the hotel hair dryer like a pro, he not only expertly dried Hannah's new golden-brown hair, but he styled it as well.

As he worked, it brought back memories and he smiled to himself. "I got to be pretty good at this before I quit," he told her, talking to her reflection in the mirror. The words seemed to come out more easily for him that way.

"Why did you quit?" Hannah wanted to know. Still without actually looking at herself, she managed to engage his eyes in the mirror.

"College," he answered simply. "I was accepted out of state and I went." Tate looked over his handiwork, reviewing what he'd done with an eye that was far more critical than the average man might be.

He'd done a damn fine job, he thought.

"I haven't cut or styled hair since then, but I guess it's like riding a bike."

The blank look in her eyes told him that Hannah probably wasn't familiar with what was to him a very old cliché. "It means that there are some things you just don't forget how to do once you learn how, no matter how much time goes by," he explained.

"Oh, I see," she said.

Finished, he removed the towel from around her neck. He couldn't take his eyes off what was at least partially his creation. "I still have it," he murmured, pleased with himself.

"It?" she questioned. She had no idea what he was referring to.

"It," he repeated, then added a definition for her benefit. "A knack." Tate could see that the explanation *still* didn't clarify anything for Hannah. She appeared to be more in the dark than ever. "In this case, the ability to cut and style hair."

She still wasn't looking at herself, he noted. That had to change.

"Go ahead," he coaxed, indicating the mirror. "Take a look. Tell me what you think."

Rather than wait for her to look up, he gently turned her head, raising it up so that it was impossible for her not to look into the mirror. Impossible for her to avoid looking at herself any longer.

Chapter 11

Bracing herself for her first look, Hannah was prepared to say something nice no matter how she felt about the image she saw looking back at her in the bathroom mirror. She was not about to hurt this man's feelings for the world and he *was* only thinking of her safety when he told her that she had to have her hair color changed, as well as cut.

What she actually wasn't prepared for was to like what she saw.

But she did.

She blinked, more than a little surprised by the appearance of the woman she saw in the mirror. It took her a few moments to take in the change, to reconcile it with what she knew she'd looked like before this extreme shift in her life.

For a minute, she couldn't take her eyes off the image looking back at her.

"Is that truly me?" she asked in a hushed whisper, as if afraid that if she spoke any louder, the image she was looking at would dissolve and just fade away.

She wasn't freaked out. Thank God, Tate thought with more than a little relief.

He stood behind her, his hands resting lightly on her shoulders, the smile on his lips spreading to his eyes and crinkling them.

"It's you, all right," he assured her. "So you don't mind what I did?" To ask her if she *liked* what he'd done might have been pushing it a little, and he didn't want her to feel he was pressuring her in any way to voice her approval. It was enough that she wasn't upset or disappointed.

"I'm pretty," Hannah said, as if she was stunned at the discovery.

Could she *really* be this free of any trace of vanity? He would have found it hard to believe—except for the fact that this was Hannah and he'd already come to know her.

"You were always pretty, Hannah," he told her. "I just gave you a different look, but your being pretty was something I had absolutely nothing to do with. It was just something I worked with."

She raised her eyes from her new reflection and looked at his instead. There was something exceedingly comforting about seeing him standing there, literally having her back—that was the correct phrase for watching over her, wasn't it? Having her back? She recalled hearing it before he'd rescued her from that terrible place. One of those awful men who was guarding them had complained that the other man "didn't have his back."

Her mouth curved in a shy smile then bloomed into

one that displayed a shade more confidence—and more than a little additional happiness.

"You are very kind, Tate."

Tate was never very comfortable about accepting gratitude. He shrugged away the words. "Just doing my job, that's all."

"It is your job to say nice things to me?" she asked as she turned around to face him. With the sink at her back and Tate standing less than a full breath away, there was precious little space for her as she turned. So she wound up brushing against him as she did so.

Tiny shock waves shot through her at all the points where her body made contact with his. Hannah drew her breath in sharply, even as her heart began to beat a little faster.

The urge to kiss her shot straight out of no-man's-land, infiltrating his system with a vengeance and making Tate acutely aware of just how attracted he was to her. It wasn't the kind of attraction a man could easily walk away from, even when common sense demanded it.

Or at least demanded that he not act on that attraction.

For one long, drawn-out moment, Tate struggled against the attraction that only seemed to send him further into this impossible situation. And then he forced himself to take a step back, even though everything in him begged him to do otherwise.

"Let's see about getting you something decent to wear," he said suddenly.

She held out the bottom of the shirt—she could just faintly catch the scent of his cologne on it and she liked that.

"I like this shirt," she told him in defense of her attire. "It feels comfortable. Roomy," she tacked on—as if she really had to.

He laughed. "It's roomy, all right. You could probably take in a family of five and hide them in that shirt," he quipped, exaggerating—but, in his opinion, not by much. And then he grinned. "I never knew a woman who didn't like to go shopping." But then, he added silently, he'd never known a woman quite like Hannah before and that made all the difference in the world. "C'mon," he beckoned, heading for the door. "Let's go."

"As you wish," she said agreeably, donning the oversize jacket he'd given her to ward off the cold when they'd escaped from his apartment.

"Give me a minute," Tate said to her once they were downstairs and about to walk past the clerk at the front desk.

Hannah nodded and wordlessly stepped off to the side as Tate exchanged a few words with the reservations clerk. The latter in turn nodded and smiled broadly.

"Thank you, sir," he said with feeling as Tate pressed something into the bald man's hand just before he rejoined her.

"Okay, let's go," Tate urged her, taking hold of her arm and guiding her across the lobby.

"Another tip?" she asked. When he looked at her quizzically, she indicated the desk clerk just before they went through the revolving door that led out to the sidewalk. "You put something in his hand and he looked very happy. I was just wondering if you gave him a tip like you did the man who brought those things to you from the store."

Tate smiled. "You're very observant," he commented, neither agreeing with nor denying her assessment of the situation.

It hadn't been a tip that he'd pressed into the man's palm. It was a cash payment for the hotel suite for another two full days. That way, it looked as if they intended to return—something he was not about to do at the end of this little impromptu shopping spree.

But he decided that now wasn't the time to go into detail about that—in case the conversation wound up being caught on camera. Although the surveillance camera might not capture sound, getting someone to watch it who had the ability to read lips was not out of the question. The Philadelphia P.D. had just such a person and there was no reason to believe that Maddox couldn't avail himself of someone with similar skills.

The whole purpose of making it look as if they were returning to the hotel was a deliberate precaution to throw Maddox and his henchmen off their trail should they have succeeded in following them this far.

Hannah said nothing in response. She might be very observant, as he said, but she was equally intuitive and her intuition told her that something was afoot again. She was just going to have to remain patient in order to determine what that "something" was.

Besides, Tate had been nothing but kind to her and she had no reason not to trust him now.

Rather than a high-end department store, like Saks or Bloomingdale's, or another shop that only carried incredibly expensive designer clothing, Tate went with his instincts and took her to Macy's on 34th Street.

He might as well have decided to take Hannah to a magic kingdom. She was utterly enchanted, not to mention somewhat overwhelmed, by the wealth of shoes, coats, dresses and other items of clothing she saw at every turn. She was accustomed to a single store commonly thought of as a general store or an emporium. For her, shopping for clothes was an endeavor that involved practicality. It wasn't undertaken to buy something "pretty." At least, not until today.

What she discovered, holding tightly on to Tate's arm as he took her from one floor to another, was such an abundance of different things to look at that she was completely mystified as to where to look first— or second or third. Her head was fairly spinning and she had to admit that part of her was convinced she was dreaming.

This was a whole new world to her. An enchanting, colorful, lovely world.

"And all this is for sale?" she asked him, finding it difficult to comprehend how there could be so many choices available. Everything came in an array of colors, styles and sizes. How did the sales personnel keep track of everything? From her point of view, it seemed like a Herculean task.

The wonder in her eyes delighted him. He could all but read her mind. "Yes, everything's for sale."

She regarded the merchandise with unabashed awe. How could she make a decision as to what to choose when each thing she picked up was even lovelier than the last? It seemed almost impossible.

"All this," she breathed almost worshipfully.

He found it difficult to suppress his grin—so he didn't.

"All this," he echoed. "C'mon," he urged her. "Let's stop looking and let's start buying you some things."

Her arm still linked through Tate's, Hannah followed

him through the maze of clothing racks and beautifully dressed mannequins that were on display.

Eventually, Tate helped her select several outfits, making sure she had more than just a couple changes of clothing. It took a while, but they amassed a wardrobe for her. After having bought her two pairs of shoes, a pair of jeans that gracefully fit her curves—unlike the jeans he'd lent her—as well as tops to go with it, plus a few skirts and dresses, he noticed Hannah fingering an ankle-length, baby-blue nightgown spun out of a light, frothy material that seemed utterly inappropriate for surviving a cold night.

But then, he mused, it was the kind of nightgown that easily created its own heat.

"Like it?" he asked her. Hannah seemed startled that he'd even noticed her looking at it. She nodded her head shyly. The next thing she knew, he gently moved her out of the way. "All right, we'll add that to the pile," he told her, removing the nightgown from its hanger. Turning around, he handed it to the saleswoman who had been discreetly hovering close by, patiently waiting for him to give some sort of sign that her services were needed.

"Oh, no," Hannah protested, a light pink color beginning to climb up her cheeks. "I couldn't let you buy that for me. It's much too..." She couldn't find the right word to explain why she couldn't accept this from him.

Watching her, Tate couldn't help getting a kick out of the fact that, after all she'd been subjected to and been through, Hannah could still blush.

He found it refreshing, compelling and—if he was being honest with himself—very sexy and alluring at the same time.

"Every woman should have something soft and feminine in her arsenal," the saleswoman told her with a confidential wink.

Somehow the wink only made her blush that much more. Flustered, Hannah looked to him, waiting for his final say in the matter. Despite the way she'd been made to dress when those men had held her and her friends captive, she thought that the nightgown was incredibly lovely, not provocative.

Did that make her a terrible person? Something inside her said no, but there were still mixed feelings warring inside of her.

Tate merely nodded at her. "It's okay," he assured her before turning toward the saleswoman. "Just pack it all up in shopping bags."

Leading the way back to the register where she'd rung up the other sales for him, the woman suggested something more convenient.

"We could have all of this delivered to your home," she told him.

For that to happen, the saleswoman was going to need an address and that was something he wasn't about to divulge. The woman was pleasant-enough looking and most likely completely innocent as well, but he was not about to take a chance. Hannah's very life was at stake. He couldn't afford to be lax or trusting. That was a luxury for another time.

"That's all right," he assured her, taking out a wad of cash to pay for the items he'd just bought, "we'll just take all of it with us."

The saleswoman nodded. "Of course," she agreed, then cheerfully invoked the classic, age-old cliché. "The customer's always right."

Hannah regarded all the things Tate had bought for her as the woman was folding the items and dividing them up between a number of shopping bags. "This is too much," Hannah protested.

"It's what you need," he countered. He picked up three shopping bags in each hand while she quickly took two more. He led the way to the down escalator. "How do you feel about walking?" he asked as they got on.

She wasn't sure what he was asking her. "I should have feelings about walking?" To her, that was just a natural part of life.

No doubt about it, Hannah was adorably charming and uncomplicated. "Let me put it another way. Are you up to walking for a while?"

She was surprised he felt the need to ask. "Yes, of course." Walking from one place to another was nothing new for her. Getting around by any other means, such as in a car, was what she wasn't accustomed to, although, she had to secretly admit, she was becoming fond of that mode of transportation.

They had reached the ground floor and he forged a path out for them. The city, always packed with people, was even more crowded with holiday shoppers trying to complete their lists.

"Good," he acknowledged. "Then we'd better get a move on. We have a bit of a trek before us."

Hannah was not quite sure what a *trek* was, but she knew that her heart told her she could follow this man anywhere and still be safe. So she nodded and walked beside him. When he tried to take her two shopping bags from her to carry himself, she refused to allow it.

"I can at least carry some of my things," she told him. After all, the shopping bags were all filled with things he'd bought for her. Not a single item in any of them was for him.

* * *

The journey through the long city blocks to their destination was slow and at times became even slower. That was because Hannah's attention would suddenly be sidetracked by the various window displays that had been deliberately decorated with an eye toward celebrating the holiday season—and to snare passing customers' attention. All the major department stores—Saks, Macy's, Bloomingdale's—were vying for sales and doing their creative best to draw people to *their* store.

Time and again Tate would realize that Hannah had suddenly stopped walking beside him and was now staring, delighted, into yet another artfully decorated window displaying another imaginative holiday scene.

Rather than being annoyed that she was throwing them off schedule, Tate found himself utterly charmed. At thirty-two, he was being granted the gift of seeing everything during the busiest time of the year for the first time because he was seeing it through Hannah's eyes. And suddenly, just like that, the cold, impersonal city had been transformed into a place of warmth and magic, because Hannah saw it that way.

It didn't mean that he lowered his guard or ceased to be alert. Tate was first and foremost a cop and thus was still very vigilant. But Hannah's joy over the different displays, each depicting some part of the holidays, was infectious and, for once, he gave no thought to resisting. She made him remember a happier time, when his parents were still alive and Christmas was spent with people who had come to mean so much to him.

"Come," Hannah coaxed as she beckoned him over

to yet another window. The shopping bags looped over her wrists, she grabbed one of his hands and pulled him to the display that had caught her attention this time.

"It's snowing inside," she marveled, then turned to him as if he could unravel all the mysteries of the world for her. She regarded him as being extremely intelligent. "How are they doing that?" she wanted to know, pointing at the snow that was gently falling to the floor behind the glass that separated her from the person inside.

There was a machine high above the display that was responsible for the light "snowfall," but to point it out to Hannah seemed a bit harsh, not to mention that the explanation came across as very mundane. Tate tapped into his imagination and said, "They squeezed a little snow cloud into the store window."

For the tiniest second, she was tempted to believe him. But she didn't. Instead, Hannah gave him a tolerant look. "You are yanking my leg."

"Pulling," he corrected, trying hard not to laugh at her phrasing. "You're pulling my leg."

Her brow furrowed as she tried to reconcile what he was saying to what he'd already done. "No, you are pulling mine."

Tickled, he began to laugh. And then he discovered he couldn't help himself. Still laughing, Tate dropped the shopping bags, leaving them huddled on either side of him as he abruptly bracketed Hannah's shoulders with his hands, leaned down and kissed her.

It was meant to be only a fleeting kiss, the most innocent of contacts. Hardly any at all. Just two pairs of lips briefly touching, simply grazing one another in quick passing.

That was all it was intended to be.

But that wasn't the way it turned out.

The kiss rocked Tate's world without warning and rocked it right down to its very core.

Chapter 12

Someone from within the crowded streets called out, "Get a room!" A high-pitched, gleeful laugh accompanied the jeer.

It was enough to jar Tate back to his senses. Annoyed, he upbraided himself for being lax enough to temporarily let his guard down.

Pulling back, he picked up the shopping bags again and murmured, "I'm sorry," to Hannah. Turning, he resumed walking toward his destination.

Stunned at the abrupt, sudden change in Tate, Hannah quickly fell into step beside him, though it was somewhat difficult, given how very crowded the streets were.

Where were all these people coming from? she couldn't help wondering. Or, for that matter, where were they going? It felt as if they belonged to some sort of a parade—except that she didn't see one underway in either direction.

"I'm not," she told him with more assertive confidence than she had displayed up to this point.

Her voice had partially been swallowed up by the din around them. He wasn't sure what she'd said. Tate glanced at her for a second. "What?"

"I'm not," she repeated, raising her voice. They stopped at the corner, waiting for the light to change. Then, just in case he didn't understand what she was referring to, Hannah raised her voice and said, "I'm not sorry that you kissed me."

"That *shouldn't* have happened," he told her with feeling.

The light turned green and the sea of people on both sides of the crosswalk moved to navigate their way to the opposite side.

"Why not?" she wanted to know.

He was impatient, but with himself, not her. He knew the rules and he was supposed to abide by them, not give in to unexpected surges of emotion. Granted, he was attracted to her, but that was *his* problem to deal with, not hers.

"Because I'm supposed to be protecting you."

She was fairly trotting beside him now, determined to keep up. And trying very hard to make sense of his reasoning.

"And you can't protect me if you kiss me?"

She wasn't making this any easier, she really wasn't, he thought. "I'm supposed to protect you, not take advantage of you."

"But you didn't take advantage of me," Hannah insisted, not understanding why he was being so hard on

himself. "You are a good man, Tate. And I *like* you."
She didn't know how to put it any better than that.

That was to be expected, given the unique circumstances. "I rescued you from a horrible situation," he said. "It's only natural for you to think you have feelings for me. But that's just gratitude, Hannah—nothing more."

The next moment, he breathed a sigh of relief. They'd gotten to their new destination without any incident. Well, without any *further* incident, he amended ruefully. He was going to have to be more careful, he warned himself.

Tate stopped for a second. Hannah had fallen half a step behind him. When she reached the canopied entrance to the high-rise building, she looked at him quizzically. Before he could say anything, a doorman dressed in navy blue livery quickly approached from the other side of the building's ornate glass door and opened it for them.

"Mr. Colton, welcome back. It's been a long time," the man said warmly, all but beaming at Tate. "Will you be staying with us long?"

"That remains to be seen, Langdon," Tate told the jovial-looking man. He wasn't about to comment on something so specific where he could be overheard by anyone. He trusted the doorman—Albert Langdon had been a fixture at the high-rise for more than the past fifteen years—but they were out in the open and any passerby could be listening to their conversation.

The doorman followed them into the marble-tiled lobby and politely relieved Hannah of the two shopping bags she was carrying.

She glanced at Tate before surrendering them and only did so after he nodded.

"I could take a few of yours, too, sir," Langdon offered. The man looked capable of easily carrying all eight of the shopping bags, as well as a couple of suitcases at the same time.

Tate crossed to the elevator. The moment he pressed the up button, the doors slid open. "That's all right, Langdon," he said, getting on. Hannah was beside him instantly. "We'll manage from here. Take the bags back, Hannah," he instructed.

She did so quickly.

Relieved of the shopping bags, the doorman retreated, tipping the brim of his hat to them as he stepped back into the lobby.

"As you wish, sir. Miss," Langdon added, nodding at Hannah.

She offered the man a shy smile, then looked at Tate the second the elevator doors closed. "This isn't the hotel."

A teasing comment about her powers of observation was on the tip of his tongue, but he had a feeling that she might think he was laughing at her. So he refrained, and responded to her statement seriously.

"No, it's not. My parents had an apartment here that they used whenever they were in New York. They left it to my brothers and sisters and me," he told her. "Now we use it when we're in town," he explained. "I thought this would be a safer place to stay than the hotel."

The elevator arrived on the twelfth floor—their floor. She had seen the button he'd pressed when they got on and knew this was the floor he wanted so when the doors opened, Hannah stepped out. She tried to ignore the queasy way her stomach felt—she didn't think she would ever get used to riding in an elevator.

She looked around for a moment, trying to get her

bearings. The walls were all carefully textured, adding a dignified richness to the surroundings.

People actually *lived* like this?

It just seemed far too grand to her for an everyday existence. But it did appeal to the artist in her.

"This is not another hotel?" she asked, unable to fathom that it might not be. She'd never seen walls quite like these.

"No, it's a high-rise apartment building."

She nodded, as if she was absorbing what he was saying, along with her surroundings. She could come to only one conclusion. "Is everyone in New York rich?" she wanted to know.

He stifled a laugh at the last minute. "No, not by a long shot," he assured her. Where had she heard that? "What makes you ask?"

"The hotel, this place, the stores—they all look so beautiful and have so much in them. I've never seen anything like this before," she confided.

She'd found herself longing for her sketchbook back home, the one she secretly kept beneath her bed and took out whenever she had a free moment to daydream. The book was filled with sketches, both drawings of nature and drawings of clothing. The latter were a product of things she'd conjured up in her head.

"This is the *real* paradise," not her village, she added silently, despite its name.

Waiting for Tate to unlock the door to the apartment he'd brought her to, Hannah set down one of the shopping bags and lightly ran her fingertips along the swirls of the textured walls.

"Beautiful," she repeated under her breath, clearly impressed by everything around her.

Tate shrugged as he pushed the door farther open

with his shoulder. He had nothing to do with either the apartment's selection or the way the hallway was decorated. Even what was inside had been decided on by his parents, or, more specifically, his mother, who had a knack for that sort of thing.

"The maid used to complain that it was a dust catcher."

Hannah's mouth curved almost wistfully as she ran her fingers along the wall again. "Still beautiful," she insisted.

Her opinion didn't change when she walked in. If anything, it just became stronger. The apartment had high ceilings and arched doorways and appeared to be completely spotless.

That kind of thing didn't just happen. Someone had been cleaning.

"Who else lives here?" she asked Tate, wondering if that person would mind her coming here unannounced like this.

For a second, he shed the bags, slipping the loops from around his wrists. He leaned the shopping bags against the wall. "No one at the moment. We all crash here when we need a place for a few days," he explained.

Hannah's expression turned to one of concern. "Crash?"

It was hard for him not to laugh. Hannah was so adorably literal-minded. He tried to put himself in her place. Tate supposed, to someone unaccustomed to slang, what he'd just said might sound confusing.

"It's an expression," he told her, then elaborated, "*Crashing* means someone coming in and staying somewhere for a few days."

Hannah was doing her best to follow what he was saying. "Ah, like a visit."

"Something like that," he allowed, then recalled a so-called friend who'd overstayed his welcome. "Except not always very pleasant."

"Not all visits are," she agreed. She remembered when Solomon Miller had attempted to return to Paradise Ridge, only to have his family turn their backs on him because he'd forsaken them for life with the *Englischers*. Solomon had been shunned. Helping those awful men kidnap her and her friends had been his way of taking revenge on his former people.

She was remembering something, Tate thought. Something disturbing. Trying to get her mind off it, he said, "C'mon, I'll show you your room."

Hannah looked at him in surprise. "I have a room here?"

He picked up the shopping bags again. All of them this time, taking four in each hand.

"Technically," he admitted, "it's one of the guest bedrooms—my parents did a lot of entertaining and they liked having people stay over."

There was warmth in his voice when he mentioned his parents, she thought. "They sound like lovely people."

"They were." And, after eleven years, he still missed them terribly.

Sympathy, as well as empathy, flooded through her. "And they are both gone now?" They had that in common, she thought.

Tate nodded. "They were in the second tower when it went down on 9/11." It occurred to him that this, too, might be conspicuously missing from her education. "Nine-Eleven, that was when—"

She stopped him by raising her hand, as if to physically halt the terrible words. "I am aware of what nine-eleven is. Paradise Ridge is not *that* isolated," she told him.

His mouth curved in a rueful smile. "Didn't mean to insult you."

"You didn't," she answered cheerfully, then, looking at him, her own mouth curved in a shy smile. "You couldn't."

He laughed then as he led the way down the hall to the bedrooms. "You're giving me entirely too much credit, Hannah."

"I think you do not give yourself enough," Hannah countered. And then she gasped as Tate pushed open the door to the room where she would be staying. "I am to stay in this room?" she asked in a hushed, almost reverent voice.

The room was most definitely decorated with a woman in mind—an exceedingly feminine woman who had a weakness for frills and throw pillows. The queen-size bed was a four-poster, complete with a white canopy and a white eyelet comforter whose edge had a pink ribbon woven through it.

It was like standing in the middle of a fairy tale, she couldn't help thinking.

Her face was the very picture of awe. He found it hard to look away. "I take it you like it."

"Like it?" she echoed. The small word didn't begin to describe how she felt. "If it were possible to be in love with something that did not breathe, then I would be in love with this room," she admitted.

Tate had absolutely no idea how to respond to that without running the risk of making her think he was making fun of her, so he directed the conversation in another, more practical direction.

"I'll just put all your things here," he told her, setting all eight shopping bags down in the corner.

She turned abruptly to face him, afraid that he was leaving. "Where will you be staying?"

"Just next door." He pointed to the bedroom next to hers. She was still afraid, he thought. And who could blame her? She'd be lucky if she didn't have nightmares about being abducted for the rest of her life. "You don't have to worry," he assured her. "I'll be right here if you need me."

Actually, he was the one who was worried, he thought. But for a completely different reason than the one he assumed she had. The proximity to Hannah's room—and Hannah—was much too close for him to be able to get a decent night's sleep and he knew it.

But again, that was his problem, not hers.

Well, he thought philosophically, he hadn't joined the Philadelphia P.D. because he'd been in search of a decent night's sleep. He had joined to make a difference and keeping Hannah safe until they caught Maddox and she testified against him was definitely going to be making a difference.

Hannah stared at the wall that separated her room from his. Envisioning Tate on the other side. Without realizing it, she ran her fingers along the outline of her lips, reliving the unexpected kiss they had shared. A kiss that made everything inside of her feel as if…as if it was waking from a deep sleep. As if she was suddenly alive in ways she couldn't have even imagined before he had kissed her.

Would he sleep peacefully? she wondered. Or would

he yearn for her? Would he stare at the wall just the way she was staring at it now?

Would he kiss her again, now that they were alone here?

Her whole body tingled from the very thought of his lips touching hers again.

And what about after? he caught himself wondering several hours later as he lay—true to his premonition—sleepless in his bed. What about after Maddox was captured, brought to trial and then put away in state prison where he belonged? Was Hannah going to be safe, going back to her own little world? Or would she need protection, just in case a member of Maddox's inner circle was still out, scot-free and biding his time until he could exact revenge on Hannah?

Would there be anyone in that village who could protect her? *Could* they even protect her, given their sheltered way of life and their feelings about violence?

One step at a time, Colton, Tate counseled himself. He needed to take this just one step at a time. If he jumped ahead of himself, he would just be needlessly driving himself crazy.

He *was* driving himself crazy.

There was no other way to describe it. Three days had passed and Seth Maddox was still out there somewhere, still at large and capable of moving in for the kill at any time.

So that meant he had to continue being Hannah's bodyguard a little longer.

And, God help him, he really liked the role. Really liked that his days and evenings were filled with Hannah and revolved entirely around her and nothing else—except for perhaps the occasional phone call he had to make, calling his supervisor, Hugo Villanueva, on a paid burner phone to find out the latest intel. He'd picked up several burner phones for just this purpose during his drive from Philadelphia to New York City.

This, as it turned out, was the closest thing he'd had to a vacation since before he began working as a detective.

Moreover, being with Hannah, day in and day out like this, forced him to view the world in softer shades and, incredibly enough, he found the more positive outlook to his liking.

He also liked that he was getting to know her better, that she was sharing things with him, such as her flair for fashion design, something that really surprised him. She did a few sketches from memory for him, showing him things she'd created "just for the fun of it." In her way of life, fashion design had no place. But her face had lit up when he'd encouraged her to keep it up.

The light in her eyes had stirred his soul long after she'd gone to bed.

He had to force himself to focus on his prime—his *only*—directive.

But being anything but constantly alert was definitely in direct conflict with the scope of his duties as her bodyguard.

She was most assuredly having an effect on him, he thought—and he liked it.

It was wrong to feel this way and he knew it. There was no denying that she was affecting his work, but there was no getting around it, he enjoyed being with her.

What he didn't enjoy were the nights when he lay on his bed, alone with his thoughts, and they tormented him. Like thinking about what his life was going to be like once she was home again.

How quickly everything had changed for him, he couldn't help but marvel. Rather than Tate making Hannah more jaded—or, in her case, just jaded—in her outlook of the world and her own future, Hannah was turning him into an optimist—and all in an astounding record three days.

Now he caught himself looking for the upside in situations rather than the downside because down situations did not generate positive outcomes.

And more than anything, Tate knew he needed a positive outcome.

Was that why he found himself wishing, fervently, that he was free, just for a little while, to act on all these incredibly urgent demands that were forever eating away at him?

Well, he couldn't act on them, he told himself sternly. He couldn't compromise her—or himself, for that matter. Since that one slip in front of the store window, he'd been trying to slowly brace himself for the inevitable future—thinking slow and steady might just be the ticket to actually winning this race.

Somehow, he was going to have to find a way to adjust to a world without her in it.

He knew it wouldn't be easy, especially since he'd backslide again. This morning, because he still hadn't made good on his promise, he finally took Hannah to see the tree in Rockefeller Center.

And her expression when she was finally able to look up at the enormous, gaily decorated Christmas tree was a sight to warm his heart. She appeared to be so captivated by it, she became almost giddy. Once she'd recovered from her sense of awe, she bombarded him with all sorts of questions about the tree and the tradition of bringing it there. She wanted to know when it had started and looked very, very impressed when he managed to answer all her questions.

He surprised himself with the amount of information he had locked away in his mind. Somewhere along the line, he reasoned, someone must have told him about this and he'd retained it.

Too bad that same someone hadn't told him what to do in order to resist the soft, compelling—and totally unwitting—allure of someone like Hannah. She came across to him as innocence personified. He knew that her captors had placed a high price on her virginity. The bidders—himself included as his other persona, he thought ruefully—were all vying for the excitement of being her "first."

To his thinking, Hannah's first time should be memorable in a good way. That meant, first and foremost, it should be with someone she really cared about, not with some sweaty pervert who'd paid top dollar for her, and secondly, it should be with someone who was around her own age, not some old man with a ton of money to throw around.

That ruled him out as well.

Granted, he wasn't an *old* man, but he *was* twelve years older than Hannah was. As far as he was concerned, that meant that the woman whose face haunted him was *way* too young for him.

Those two reasons should have been enough to harness any and all his stray thoughts, as well as all the urges that seemed to be mercilessly and ceaselessly battering his body.

All that was more than logical and reasonable. After

all, he prided himself on being a logical and reasonable guy.

So why was it that he couldn't make himself remember any of those reasons for more than a few seconds at a time?

Chapter 13

The rustling noise barely registered on the perimeter of his consciousness.

But it was enough.

Tate sat up, instantly awake and alert, straining to make out the sound he believed he'd just heard. For a second, there was nothing.

Had it just been his imagination, or was there someone moving around in his apartment?

And then he heard it again.

Rustling.

Movement.

There was definitely someone out there.

Tate was out of bed and on his feet, the weapon he kept beneath his pillow in his hand and ready to fire before another two seconds had elapsed.

Mindful of not making any noise that would alert whoever was there, Tate slowly turned his doorknob and eased the door open in what felt like slow motion. He started to look around. The moment he did, he saw her.

Hannah.

Her body language told him that she was completely at ease and she wouldn't have been if there was someone else in the apartment with them.

She might have been at ease, but he certainly wasn't. Not from the moment he realized what she had on.

He could feel every fiber of his body come to rigid attention and hold its collective breath.

Hannah was wearing the nightgown she'd wistfully pointed out to him during the shopping spree he'd taken her on.

She was wearing the nightgown and nothing else.

The moonlight that had entered, uninvited, through the bay window and was painting everything in the room in soft, golden hues, was doing the very same thing along the outline of her body.

If Tate hadn't known that it was impossible, he would have sworn that he'd come precariously close to swallowing his own tongue at the very sight of her.

He knew that the temperature around him had gone up at least twenty degrees—if not more.

Belatedly, he lowered his gun and drew in an inordinately large breath. Only then was he able to ask her, "What are you doing up at this hour?"

Hannah almost jumped as she turned around to face him. "I'm sorry. I didn't mean to wake you," she told him. Her expression was the most sincerely apologetic one he'd ever seen on a person.

"Don't worry about it." He forced himself to look only at her face. Even so, Tate could feel his body temperature rising even more as she began to drift toward him. "I sleep with one eye open anyway—occupational habit," he added with a self-deprecating smile. "Why can't you sleep?"

"Worried, I guess." She raised her eyes to his and the part of him that wasn't overheating was absolutely mesmerized. "And restless," she added. "I feel as if I don't know what to do with myself."

"Well, given the hour, I think the logical suggestion would be to go to bed." He did his best to keep his voice steady, but it was getting more and more difficult just to concentrate on what he was saying and not on the woman he was saying it to.

Especially since she had somehow managed to get so close to him, he could feel her breathing.

"Hannah," he began, his throat closing so tight he was less than one step away from gasping out the rest of the words.

Her eyes never left his and he felt as if he was drowning in them.

"Yes?" she whispered.

He was digging his fingernails into his palms now, trying to distract himself any way he could. It wasn't working.

"Didn't we get a robe to go with that?"

"No." She thought a minute, then shook her head. "I did not see one hanging next to it. Why?" She looked down at the clinging nylon, then back up at him. "You don't like it?"

If anyone else had asked the question, he would have said it was an out-and-out calculated attempt at seduction. But this was Hannah asking, and it came out as just another innocent question.

The trouble was, he was *not* having an innocent reaction to the question, to her *or* to the nightgown. Highlighted as it was by the moonlight, it was the last word in transparent and consequently left absolutely *nothing* to the imagination.

Just as well since, in this particular case, his imagination couldn't have begun to do her the kind of justice she actually deserved.

Nothing he could have conjured up held a candle to what he saw now.

He had to tread lightly here because he was picking his way through land mines that could go off at any second at the slightest misstep.

"It's not a matter of not liking it—I do," he assured her with feeling. "It's a matter of trying to remember that I'm the one who is supposed to make sure no harm comes to you."

Hannah seemed to be able to see between the lines and hear what he *wasn't* saying. "You wouldn't harm me," she told him with the certainty that only belonged to the pure and the innocent.

"I wouldn't be so sure, if I were you," he said as he continued to struggle with himself, trying his best to ignore the very real ache as well as the breathless passion that were all but running wild throughout his entire body.

Sainthood, he thought. He was definitely a candidate for sainthood if he managed to walk away from this and leave her untouched.

"But I am," she told him. "Just as I am sure that you are a good man and that you make me feel very, very safe." Her eyes were open wide, as if her very soul was communing with his. "And I still mean what I said the other day. Except that I no longer just like you. I love you."

She reached up to touch his face and he caught her hand in his.

That, it turned out, was his first mistake.

"Hannah, you don't—"

He didn't get a chance to finish because she closed the last bit of space between them and now her body was against his, creating sharp arrows of desire that instantly shot all through him.

"Hannah, don't," he whispered, struggling against what he was feeling. Struggling not just against himself, but against her as well.

He was a man destined to fail and he knew it. Even so, he was not about to surrender his conscience without a fight.

"Don't what?" she whispered, taking his hand and placing it on her small, perfect breast. The moment she did, she drew in a long breath, igniting at the point of contact.

Her heart began to hammer wildly—he could feel it beneath his palm.

Tate tried to pull his hand back, but the light pressure from hers was enough to keep it just where it was. He was forced to fight not just his own desires, but hers as well, and he knew that he was badly outnumbered— and pretty much doomed to fail.

"Oh, Hannah," he groaned just before the last of his defenses crumbled and he capitulated. "I'm sorry," he whispered as he framed her face in his hands.

Just as when he'd kissed her for the first time, she told him, "I'm not," and meant it.

Any sliver of hope Tate might have had of rallying and pulling away from her and his own consuming desires vanished in that moment.

Tate had no choice but to bring his mouth down on

hers. The second he did, he succumbed to the very taste of her.

When she rose on her toes, lacing her arms around his neck and pressing her body against his as she kissed him back, Tate lost all ability to think, to reason, to hold himself in check. All he could possibly hope for was to be able to give her a small measure of the sheer pleasure she'd created within him with that incredibly delectable mouth of hers.

The rest all took place in a swirling haze that infiltrated his head.

Scooping Hannah up in his arms, his lips still sealed to hers, Tate carried her into his bedroom and set her down on his bed. The moment he did, he lay down beside her and proceeded—with great care—to open up a brand-new world to her.

Just as she, with her eager innocence, questing fingertips and unknowingly wicked mouth, opened up one for him.

Hannah wasn't altogether sure what made her so very bold or why she knew that, after all this time of being reserved and guarded with men, this was right, but she did.

Just as she knew in her soul that Tate was the one man she was meant to be with, meant to give herself to, and that it was all right. That what she was doing was right, even if there were no vows to sanction it, no ring on her finger. Right, despite the fact that he was not one of her own people, but an outsider.

It didn't matter. None of it mattered.

What she was feeling defied definition and was too great to be confined within such narrow things as traditions and timeless rules. She loved him and yearned for him beyond all understanding, beyond the borders of sanity.

Something had told her the first time she'd felt his hand on her arm that he was the one and that they belonged together. Together for a day, a year, for a lifetime—together for however long it was destined to be.

And should their paths be suddenly pulled apart, she knew she was going to love him until the last breath was gone from her body—and quite possibly beyond that.

So it was with something comparable to sheer abandonment that she threw herself into Tate's embrace, that she absorbed every pass of his lips along her skin, every caress of his hand along her flesh.

Abandonment yielded a euphoric ecstasy.

There were things happening to her, things a girl raised the way she had been hadn't even begun to dream about or imagine. Wonderful, delightful things that felt like intoxicating, blissful explosions all throughout her body.

She didn't know where to race within her mind in order to absorb everything, cherish everything.

It overwhelmed her.

Until he suddenly caught her hand, stopping her.

She looked at him, wide-eyed and confused. "Am I doing it wrong?" she asked.

"No, you're doing it right. Too right," he told her. He wasn't ready for the final ascent and if she'd touched him like that one more time, she would have made it begin.

The darkest, hottest and deepest spot in hell had been officially reserved for him when he died and he knew it. He was afraid he didn't have the will or the power to stop himself.

Only Hannah could do that and she wasn't stopping him.

With every twist and turn of her body, every sound that came from her lips, she was doing the exact opposite. She was urging him on.

He caught her hands a second time and she looked at him, dazed and confused.

"No, Hannah, we can't do this."

"What's wrong?" she asked in a small, puzzled voice. "Don't you want me?"

"Not want you?" he repeated. "Oh, God, I've never wanted *anything* as much as I want you."

"Then I don't understand. Why wouldn't you do this? Why won't you make love to me?"

"Because it has to happen the right way. Not here, not on the run. It should be a feast, not a snack. Your first time should be memorable—a banquet, not a sandwich snatched up in haste." He pressed a kiss to her forehead and held her to him, his own heart racing as he struggled to bank down his chaotic emotions. "You deserve the best of everything," he told her.

She raised her head, her eyes meeting his. "I have it right here," she whispered, her meaning clear. And then she smiled up at him. "You are a good man, Tate. A noble man."

"That's me, noble," he echoed, doing his best to rouse his sense of honor and use it to smother the smoldering embers of his desire.

"Would it be too much to ask you to sleep in my bed with me?"

"Hannah—" he began with a warning note.

"Just to sleep," she emphasized. "I would feel safer."

"I really don't think—"

"In my village, people who are to be married do it.

They have a bundling board between them so that each stays on his or her side of the bed."

And no one ever leaped over the board, right? he thought sarcastically. But she looked so earnest that when she followed her request with "Please," he couldn't bring himself to turn her down.

"All right," he said reluctantly, in his heart knowing that this would be the biggest challenge he had ever met.

They had no board, so they used an old broom he found shoved into the pantry, laying it between them on her bed.

Hannah fell asleep almost immediately.

Tate did not.

Instead, resigned to a sleepless night, he watched as she slept. And somewhere in the middle of the night, it occurred to him that if he actually were capable of loving anyone, Hannah would have been the one he loved.

Chapter 14

Hannah woke up slowly, by degrees, reluctant to abandon the comforting embrace of sleep. Afraid of what she might find when she was awake.

The kidnapping had done that to her, stolen her peace of mind, thrown her headlong into a world where she did not belong. Shown her the brutality of life. Robbed her of her natural bent toward pure happiness without hesitation.

When she finally opened her eyes to find Tate next to her, propped up on his elbow and just looking down at her, a bemused smile curving his mouth, a sense of relief washed over her. Last night *hadn't* been a dream and its effects burst on her mind all over again.

And once it did, the expression on her face matched his.

"Good morning," she murmured softly, stretching beneath the blanket.

Though she was covered, Tate could clearly make out the outline of her body. Make it out and feel himself responding to her all over again.

Damn, but he didn't recognize himself, not even a little. This new person he'd become was in love with a woman he hadn't even made love to. How the hell had that happened anyway? Granted, sex had never been a driving force for him. He'd always enjoyed the intimacies with women, then moved on because there was so much else going on in his life.

The prime elements in his life were, and had always been, his family and his career. Finding someone to share his bed—and, ultimately, his life—had never once been a priority with him—or even a distant third.

If he were being completely honest about the subject, had it turned out that he was never to find the right woman to spend his life with, well, he wouldn't have felt incomplete. There was so much else to occupy his time and his mind.

But one night with Hannah—just watching her sleep for God's sake—had changed his resolute position—and he couldn't even say why. He just knew that it had. *Knew* that he would do whatever it took to keep Hannah safe. And that, if he could, he would keep her in his life for as long as he feasibly could before letting her go back to her world.

Not that he wanted to keep Hannah against her will, because he cared far too much about her to do that to her. But if she seemed the least ambivalent about going back, he would do what he could to persuade her to remain in his world, rather than to return to the quaint world she'd always known.

With a slow, light movement, he brushed aside the lock of hair that had fallen into her eyes.

"Good morning, yourself." He could go on looking at her like this forever, Tate thought and for a moment, wished that circumstances were such that he could. "Did you sleep well?"

She smiled and nodded. "Very well, thank you." He noted that there was nothing shy or withdrawn about her smile anymore. It was the smile of a woman who was confident about the brand-new world she'd been initiated into.

Hannah stretched again, more languidly this time, and he felt himself losing ground fast. "You keep doing that and I'm going to forget all about getting up."

A delighted laugh escaped her lips as she deliberately stretched again, this time watching his eyes as she did so. There was mischief in her own.

Suddenly pulling her to him so that her body fit against his, Tate told her, "You have no one to blame for this but yourself."

"I'll try to remember that," she answered, doing her best to look solemn. She didn't even come close to succeeding.

The next moment, there was no more time for talking as she sank into his kiss.

It took them almost two hours before they finally were dressed and able to leave the apartment. Both hungry, Tate was taking her out for breakfast. Hannah had protested the need to go out, saying that she was more than happy—and willing—to cook for him. He stuck to his original plan, saying that he didn't want her to feel obligated to wait on him in any manner.

"You have all the time in the world to stand over a hot stove when you go back to your village," he told her. "You deserve to enjoy being spoiled a little."

She inclined her head in agreement, saying nothing.

She felt a little guilty about it, but right now, she didn't want to think about going home. She dearly loved her brother and his family and there was no denying that she missed them, but there was something wonderfully alluring about New York City and the world that Tate had opened up for her. Though she knew she didn't really belong in it, she wanted to be able to "visit" it for just a little while longer.

When they came downstairs to the foyer, Hannah nodded a greeting at the doorman on duty, but the main focus of her attention was the man whose arm she'd slid her own through.

The heavyset man offered them a cheery "Good morning, Mr. Colton. Good morning, miss," as he held the door open for them.

Hannah huddled against Tate's arm as a blast of cold December air greeted them the second they came out of the building.

"We'll take a cab," Tate decided, raising his hand to catch the attention of the next passing cabdriver.

"Oh, no. Please, let's walk," Hannah urged. She wanted to savor every moment she had with him. "I don't mind the cold."

He dropped his hand just as a cab pulled up before them. Shaking his head, he dismissed the driver. "The lady's changed her mind."

The cabbie mumbled something under his breath as he drove away.

He'd almost walked right into them, but as recognition suddenly hit him, the heavyset man managed to sidestep out of the way at the last minute.

Talk about dumb luck, Darren Sorell, the man who considered himself Maddox's right-hand man, thought.

He stared after the couple he'd almost plowed into. They were going down the block now.

He'd been looking for the woman, Jade, for the past five days, ever since that raid on the warehouse had taken place and all the high rollers had scattered like frightened mice, trying to abandon a sinking ship.

Only a handful of Maddox's men—Maddox included—had managed to escape. And Maddox didn't want to leave behind any loose ends. Jade was a loose end. A very big loose end. Unlike the other girls who'd been taken from that backward, medieval village where they lived, according to Maddox, Jade had been an unwitting witness to things that would put him away for the rest of his life.

The way around that was to find her and eliminate the threat.

Sorell had been the unlucky one to draw the assignment and he'd been combing the city ever since someone had said that the last call from the so-called high roller who had been so interested in Jade at the warehouse party had been traced back to New York City.

It looked like the tip had paid off.

Snow was beginning to fall. Sorell took shelter in the doorway of a coffee shop that had recently gone out of business. Taking out his cell phone, he immediately called Maddox to report the sighting.

The second he heard the phone stop ringing, he announced, "I found her. She chopped off her hair and dyed what's left, but it's her. There's no mistaking that face."

"Where?" Maddox bit off.

"Coming out of a fancy high-rise in the city. Building's got a doorman and—"

Maddox cut him short. "Anyone with her?"

"Yeah, that guy from the warehouse party, the one who was slobbering over her."

Maddox uttered a curse. "That wasn't a guy, that was the undercover cop, you idiot."

Used to his boss's lack of gratitude and surly temper, Sorell shrugged to himself. "Yeah, right. Now I remember. All I know was that he was sticking to her like glue."

"Plant yourself outside the high-rise," Maddox ordered. "The second he 'unglues' himself and goes somewhere without her, you know what to do."

"What if he doesn't? Unglue himself," Sorell elaborated when there was no reply on the other end.

"Then kill them both," Maddox snapped. "Do I have to do your thinking for you, too?"

Before Sorell could answer, the connection was terminated.

"Sure thing, boss," Sorell said sarcastically into the phone as if he were still talking to the other man. Frowning, he tucked his cell phone back into his pocket and stepped out of the doorway.

He was going to be out here a long time, he thought. He had no illusions about his boss. If Sorell came back before he carried out the man's orders, Maddox would have him killed.

"If I told you something, would you promise not to think badly of me?" Hannah ventured nearly two hours later as they were walking back from the restaurant where they'd had breakfast and then lingered over their second cups of coffee.

Tate laughed and shook his head. Everything about this woman was endearing. "I don't think it's possible to think badly of you."

She blushed in response and he watched her skin take on a rosy tint. He felt his heart swell again. She had that effect on him.

"I like it here," she confided in a low voice, as if what she was sharing with him was a secret. "I think I would like to stay a little longer."

No more than I'd like you to stay, he thought, silently cheering. But he managed not to give himself away as he said out loud, "Well, right now, there's not much of a choice," he answered. "Despite the number of people around us, it's easier keeping tabs on who's coming and going here in New York than if you were hiding in a small town."

"A small town like mine," she guessed.

He nodded. "Like yours."

Maybe, Tate thought, just maybe, since she seemed to be settling in for now, he could find a way to convince her to remain with him for a while longer. A *lot* longer, he amended.

He knew he shouldn't be getting his hopes up, that someone as sheltered, as pure, as Hannah should go back to her family and friends as soon as possible, but he couldn't help wishing that she wouldn't. That she'd want to stay with him.

Get a grip, Colton. You know the score, she doesn't. She's better off with her own kind.

Knowing he was right didn't make it any easier to accept.

He had no sooner walked into the apartment with Hannah than he heard his cell phone ringing.

This can't be good, he thought, though his expression gave nothing away when Hannah looked at him quizzically.

Pressing his lips together to keep from frowning, Tate took his cell phone out and looked down at the caller ID.

Nope, this isn't going to be good, he thought.

It wasn't some random call, or a call from his sister, asking for an update. Instead, the call was coming in from his supervisor.

Hugo Villanueva rarely called his people himself, preferring to delegate tasks as well as responsibility whenever he saw fit. That he was the one calling meant that something was up.

"Colton," Tate said as he took the call. Out of the corner of his eye, he saw Hannah watching him apprehensively. His body language must have given him away. He deliberately smiled at her, hoping to erase the worried furrows from her forehead.

Hoping to do the same for himself.

As with all his calls, this call was short and to the point. Villanueva was calling an impromptu meeting and wanted all hands on deck, including him. Tate looked at Hannah uncertainly as his supervisor gave him last-minute instructions.

He didn't like the idea of leaving Hannah alone— but there was no one he could leave her with while he attended this unscheduled meeting.

When he heard Villanueva pause, Tate said, "I'll do my best to be there."

"Don't 'do your best,' just be there," Villanueva ordered just before he ended the call.

The man could use a few tips on sociability, Tate thought, putting his cell phone away.

The call over, Hannah was instantly beside him. She searched his face. "Is something wrong?"

He knew better than to brush her off with a trite "No,

of course not." "That was my supervisor. He wants to have everyone who's working on this case come in for a meeting."

"Yes?" There was a question in her voice, as if she knew there was more and she was coaxing him to continue.

He sighed, tamping down his agitation. "And I can't bring you with me."

She continued looking at him, waiting for him to say something that explained the look on his face. "And?"

"And I don't like leaving you alone," he ground out. Leaving her unattended went against all his instincts.

Hannah smiled patiently, placing a gentling hand on his shoulder. For now, their roles had reversed and she was the reassuring one. "I'm not a child, Tate. I know how to lock the door. And I won't open it," she added, sensing he needed to hear her assure him of that. "Go to your meeting with your supervisor. Hear what he has to tell you. I will be fine," she stressed with a warm smile.

He wasn't convinced. This was making him extremely uneasy, as if he was going against his better judgment. "I don't know—"

Handing him his overcoat, Hannah began pushing him toward the door.

"I do," she insisted. "Go. I will be right here, waiting for you."

He supposed maybe he was overreacting and worrying too much. After all, there *was* a doorman in front of the building, and Langdon never allowed anyone in unless he either knew the person, or one of the tenants could vouch for the guy. No stranger was going to get by him.

Putting his overcoat back on, he turned to look at Hannah. If anything happened to her, he wouldn't be able to live with himself. "And you promise you won't open the door?"

She held her hand up solemnly, making a pledge. "I promise I won't even come near the door until I see you walking across the threshold."

"I guess that'll have to do," he said. His hand on the doorknob, Tate paused long enough to kiss Hannah soundly. "I'll be back as soon as I can."

"And I will be here, waiting," she promised. She closed the door behind him, then flipped the locks just the way he'd showed her.

She started to walk away, then stopped. Intuition told her that Tate was still there, on the other side of the door. She doubled back.

"Go!" she ordered through the door with a laugh.

"All right," she heard Tate say through the door. "Stay safe."

"You, too," she answered, raising her voice so that he could hear. "You, too."

Giving it to the count of ten, she waited for any further indication that Tate was still hovering in the hallway.

When there was nothing further, she smiled to herself and went into the kitchen. By the time Tate came back, he'd probably be hungry and she didn't want him to feel they had to go out to another one of the restaurants that seemed to be absolutely everywhere she looked.

There had to be *something* in this kitchen that she could use to make if not an exciting meal, at least a nourishing one.

A ten-minute search through the refrigerator and the pantry told her that she just might be wrong about that. She was still foraging through the vast cupboard space when she thought she heard the front door opening again.

At this rate, the man was never going to get to his meeting. With a shake of her head, she laughed. "What's your excuse for coming back this time?" she wanted to know.

"Didn't know I needed one."

She stiffened as every hair on the back of her neck stood up. The deep voice didn't belong to Tate, but she still recognized it.

She felt sick.

The voice belonged to one of the other guards who came into the motel on occasion. He was the one who made her skin crawl every time he looked at her. There was something exceedingly humiliating about the way his eyes swept over her.

They'd found her.

Frantic, Hannah looked around for some way to escape, or, barring that, somewhere to hide.

Hannah remembered that she and Tate had escaped from his apartment in Philadelphia by climbing up those iron stairs that ran the length of the building. She hadn't seen any of those stairs on the front of the building, but maybe they were located on the other side, like by the bedroom window.

She made a quick dash for the bedroom, but her escape was abruptly cut short before it could fully get underway. The husky, bald man, moving incredibly quickly for a man of his girth, grabbed her before she could make it out of the room.

Unlike when she'd been abducted from Paradise Ridge, Hannah fought back this time. Fought using her nails, her fists, her legs, anything she could. She was a whirling dervish, scratching, punching, kicking and biting.

Because she'd surprised him by resisting in this fierce manner, Hannah managed to escape from him when she kicked him where it did the most painful good.

Sorell cursed at her roundly as he howled in pain. Hannah darted out of the room, heading for the bedroom.

Knowing he couldn't come back without her, Sorell managed to rally and he caught her by her hair, yanking her back.

The movement was so abrupt, it was all she could do not to scream as pain shot first through her scalp and then through every inch of her. Turning her around, he punched her in the face.

Battered, with her head spinning badly, Hannah fought back like a tiger. It was then, just as she thought she could get free, that she felt the sharp prick of a needle going into the side of her neck.

Instantly, her limbs felt as if they had turned into tree trunks, completely weighing her down. She couldn't move and she was struggling to keep her eyes open, to remain conscious.

It was a battle she was destined to lose.

She thought she heard the bald man talking to someone, but she couldn't turn her head to see who.

The next moment, her surroundings faded to black and then completely disappeared.

Chapter 15

Well, those were two hours of his life he was never going to get back again, Tate thought as he made his way back to the building where he was staying. The meeting, in his opinion, hadn't really been necessary. No new information had surfaced, only a rehashing of what he already knew and suspected that Villanueva *knew* that he knew.

All right, he amended, turning down the next block and narrowly avoiding a dog walker and his Doberman, that wasn't entirely true. No new *helpful* information had surfaced. What had come to light was that several more bodies of abducted young women had been found.

Tate suppressed a sigh. This was going to upset Hannah. He knew she identified with them.

He dreaded telling her, but he didn't see a way around that. He wasn't going to lie to her or keep anything from her. If he did, he risked losing her trust, which he was *not* about to do. He just needed to pick the right time to tell her, he thought, and that wasn't going to be easy.

The distant sound of a siren splintered his thoughts.

The sound grew closer and he looked over his shoulder in time to see an ambulance, its lights flashing wildly, coming down the block.

There was no reason in the world that seeing it should make him suddenly grow apprehensive. It wasn't as if an ambulance, flying by traffic, was an uncommon sight in Manhattan. At any given moment, there were eight million people in the city with a great many of those people stuffed into every square block. The ambulance could have been summoned by any one of them for reasons that had nothing to do with Hannah.

He pulled over, parked the car and broke into a run anyway, heading straight for the high-rise building where he'd left her.

The feeling of dread and anxiety tripled the moment he saw the ambulance double-park right in front of his building.

The next moment, as he came closer to the building, he saw that Langdon was missing from his post.

Did that mean the doorman was inside, tending to whoever the ambulance had come for?

Oh, God, don't let it be Hannah.

Still running, Tate finally reached the front door. The paramedics were already inside. Yanking the door open, he could see one of them kneeling over someone.

Fear all but strangled him.

I should have never left her, Tate silently upbraided himself. *Why the hell didn't I go with my instincts and take her with me?*

"Is she—?" The question died abruptly on his lips

as he came to a halt directly behind the kneeling paramedic. The body on the ground wasn't Hannah.

It was the doorman.

Langdon lay unconscious in a pool of his own blood. There was so much blood, it outlined the upper part of his torso. The paramedic was feeling for a pulse.

"It's thin, but it's there," he told his partner. And then he saw Tate. "Move back, buddy, and let us do our job," he ordered impatiently. "You can look on from the sidelines."

Tate didn't bother mentioning that he was a cop. He was moving too fast. There was only one reason anyone would try to eliminate Langdon: they didn't want a witness.

The lobby began to fill with tenants. Tate raced past all of them. The elevator was in use. Rather than wait, he took the stairs.

Tate didn't remember running up all those flights to his floor. He was only aware of praying.

By the time he finally reached his floor, his legs felt like rubber—disembodied rubber. He couldn't feel his feet and he wasn't sure just how he did it, but he managed to cross the hallway to his apartment.

There wasn't even an attempt to hide his tracks. The gunman had left the apartment door wide open.

The living room was a shambles. With its overturned table, scattered books and broken figurines—the figurines he'd given her as souvenirs of their night on the town—giving clear testimony that a fight had taken place here just within the two hours he'd been gone.

Hannah hadn't gone quietly with her abductor.

Had to have been one hell of a surprise to whoever had been sent to get her. She'd gone from a docile, meek young woman who gave herself less rights than her shadow to a woman of spirit who couldn't be easily overcome.

He took comfort in the fact that Hannah had to be still alive. If Maddox had merely wanted her dead, Tate knew he would have been looking down at her body right now, not the aftermath of a battle.

Okay, *they'd* taken her—but taken her where?

Looking around his apartment, he hadn't a clue.

It had to be a place where Maddox felt he had the advantage over whoever might come looking for him—or for Hannah.

Tate tried to think if there was anyone who would have been privy to that kind of information. But fear for Hannah's safety was undermining his ability to think clearly.

He took a deep breath, ordering himself to calm down, to look at this as if it was just another case to be solved and resolved with optimal results.

But it *wasn't* just another case, dammit. Hannah's life was at stake and he couldn't afford to be wrong, couldn't afford to fail.

Hurrying out of the apartment, he didn't even bother to close the door. Instead, he pulled his cell phone out and called the only person he trusted right now.

Emma answered on the third ring. "Colton."

"Emma, they took her."

She'd attended the meeting with Villanueva as well and hadn't expected to hear from her brother so soon. As it was, she could barely make out his voice.

"Tate? Is that you? Where are you, you're breaking up."

He raised his voice, exasperated at the reception and far more exasperated with himself. He should have never left Hannah alone.

"I'm in the stairwell at the high-rise. That meeting with Villanueva, Maddox used the opportunity to have Hannah kidnapped again. The apartment's in shambles."

Emma took that as a good sign. "That means she tried to fight them off. She's still alive, Tate."

But for how long? "She knows too much," he said, taking the next flight down. "Maddox is going to kill her."

Emma searched for slivers of hope to offer her brother, as well as Caleb when she told him about this newest development. "Maybe not. If that's all he wants, then he would have done it already."

"And maybe he wants to make an example of her to the others," Tate countered. Even as he said it, he felt sick to his stomach. Maddox was going to torture Hannah, *then* kill her—he was sure of it. "I've got to find her before that happens, Emma."

"*We'll* find her, Tate," his sister told him with as much confidence as she could muster. He didn't need to hear the actual odds against that right now. Besides, miracles happened every day—they just needed one. And this was the season for them, she told herself.

Reaching the ground floor, he pushed open the door leading from the stairwell. "Who would have any idea where Maddox would take her?"

Emma tried to think. "Anyone who'd know is already dead. The people we arrested at the raid are just grunt-level henchmen—"

Before him, in the lobby, Tate saw that the paramedics had just finished strapping Langdon to the gurney. Pale and bleeding, the wounded doorman had apparently regained consciousness, which was a good sign,

Tate thought. The paramedics were going to be taking the man to the hospital—

"Hospital," Tate suddenly said out loud as an idea hit him.

"What about a hospital?" Emma asked, confused.

"What hospital did they take Miller to after the raid?" He knew that the informant had been shot, but lucky for him, the bullet had gone straight through and, despite a large loss of blood, the formerly disgraced member of the Amish community was going to make it.

"Let me think." Emma paused, then said, "Philadelphia General was the closest one to the warehouse. They'd have taken him there."

"He still there?" he asked eagerly. Miller was the only one he knew to question. The man had known all the ins and outs of Maddox's operation from the first kidnapping. Maybe he'd have an idea where the man would take Hannah.

"As far as I know," Emma qualified before saying, "yes."

"Then that's where I'm heading. Call the hospital, have them double the guard. Maddox might have gotten it into his head to clean house."

It was an educated guess, but Tate was reasonably certain he was right. A man like Maddox, who saw himself above the people he dealt with, would easily kill Miller without so much as a passing qualm.

It was ninety-seven miles from the heart of New York City to Philadelphia, a trip that, on a good day with traffic permitting, could be made in just a little under two hours.

Calling in favors, he managed to get his hands on a NYPD detective's car, complete with portable flashing lights, and Tate made the trip in a little over an hour. He spent the entire ride trying his best to calm down, but it was no use. He was highly agitated, highly wired and praying he wasn't already too late.

Hannah had trusted him to protect her and he'd failed in his assignment.

He'd failed *her*.

If anything happened to her, he'd never forgive himself. If that madman so much as—

Tate stopped. He couldn't let himself think about anything except getting her back. It had to be his entire focus. Otherwise, he'd be no good to anyone, least of all to Hannah.

Reaching the hospital, he made his way upstairs then hurried down the surgical unit hallway to ICU, the area where Miller was being kept. While the man technically was not under arrest, he was still a prisoner in his room. There was an armed guard posted right outside his door, cautiously watching the movements of every approaching person with a wary eye.

Tate took out his badge and held it up for the guard to check. "Detective Tate Colton. I need to talk to Miller," he told the man.

Nodding, the guard stepped to the side to allow him access to the room.

The moment Tate walked in, the listless look on Miller's face vanished. "You here to spring me?" the man asked hopefully.

Tate didn't bother answering the question. Every second counted and he had an anxious feeling that there weren't very many left.

He led with his reason for being there. "Maddox's got Hannah Troyer."

Miller looked at him, confused. "I thought you rescued her—"

"I did. He kidnapped her again," Tate bit off. His
tone left no room for a discussion. "Where would he
take her? We've got people watching all his known
hangouts." Emma had taken care of that for him, sending out extra agents to cover Maddox's former haunts.
"And he hasn't shown up at any of them. Is there any
place, some secret hideout maybe, or a place that means
something to him, that he'd go to?"

Miller thought for a second, then bobbed his head
up and down like one of those annoying big-headed
dolls people kept insisting on putting in the rear of
their vehicles.

"He's got this place where he'd take the girls whenever he was getting ready to get rid of them. He called
it the Kill House." Miller raised his eyes to Tate's face.
"It's this abandoned boathouse just off the Allegheny
River." Miller's voice grew quiet. "That was where he
took those girls whose bodies I led your sister and Hannah's brother to. He killed them himself. He got off on
the life-and-death power trip," Miller added with an
involuntary shiver.

The boathouse.

That had to be it.

It was a gamble, Tate admitted, but it was one hand
he was going to have to play until the end. "Tell me
how to get there," he ordered Miller.

With Miller's directions freshly embedded in his
mind—as well as into the GPS in the car he was using,
Tate drove on the expressway as if the very devil were
behind him in hot pursuit.

But the devil wasn't after him, he thought wryly.

He was actually on his way *to* the devil. And fervently praying that he would get there in time. Because if Maddox had killed her—hell, if he'd harmed a single hair on Hannah's head, Tate couldn't be held responsible for what he'd do to the black-hearted bastard.

He *had* to be on time, Tate prayed over and over again, he just *had to be.*

"What is this place?" Hannah asked, looking around, doing her very best not to sound as frightened as she really was.

"The last place you'll ever see," Maddox told her nastily. "Gotten real chatty since the last time, haven't you?" he mocked. "That undercover cop do that for you? Teach you how to run off at the mouth? What else did he do? Make you a lot of promises that if you testify against me, wonderful things were going to happen to you? Bet you didn't count on this being one of those 'things,'" he jeered. "Did you?"

His laugh sent a chill zigzagging down her spine, forming icicles along its way. Somehow, Hannah still continued to hold her head up.

"You're an evil man and you have to be stopped," she told him hotly. He was responsible for her friends being killed. She remembered now, remembered it clear as day, and her anger rose to a dangerous level.

He laughed shortly. "Maybe so, but not today, sweetheart. And not by the likes of you, that's for damn sure." His eyes narrowed as he looked at her. "Dead men tell no tales—it's a trite saying, but it's accurate. And it applies to dead whores, too."

The moment they came to the dilapidated building, she braced her hands on either side of the doorway, refusing to enter. Cursing, he pushed her hard through the open doorway. Hannah found herself stumbling into the old, abandoned single-story structure. Inches away from her foot, a rat scurried away.

Hannah swung around to face him. "Why are you doing this?" she cried.

The condescending sneer on his face deepened and he laughed. The sound made her skin crawl. "Because I can, my dear. Because I can."

Hannah knew that her ways were completely different from this man's, but she still couldn't understand his reasoning. Why would he risk everything he'd worked for to kill her, not to mention her friends and the other Amish girls? "But you have so much to lose."

"Leaving you alive isn't going to change that," he told her. "But it will teach that bastard, Colton, that he can't mess with me and not suffer consequences for his actions." His eyes seemed to bore right into her, pinning her in place. "The same goes for you. Now," he took a deep breath as he stepped toward her, "not that this hasn't been interesting, but I really have somewhere else to be so—let me take care of this loose end and I can be on my way."

The next moment, moving so quickly that had she blinked, she would have missed it, Maddox had his hands around her throat.

Startled, Hannah tried to back away as she pushed her hands hard against his chest. But she couldn't budge him. There was no way.

His hands were tightening around her throat, cutting off her air supply.

Frantic now, knowing she only had seconds left, Hannah started to claw at Maddox's face. She raked her nails down his cheeks, then tried to stick her finger into his eye, hoping to create enough sudden pain to make him drop his hands from her throat.

Rather than push her hands away, he just continued doing what he was doing. Squeezing harder.

Hannah felt her strength quickly being sapped away. She didn't know how much longer she could last, how much longer she could keep trying to resist.

It couldn't end like this, she thought, flashes of heat exploding through her brain so that holding on to thoughts was proving to be very difficult.

She didn't want to die. Not when she was just on the brink of this wonderful new world that Tate had shown her. She wanted to live, to be with him. To make him happy that he'd saved her.

To make him happy…

The pain was awful and her grasp on the world was beginning to swiftly fade away.

She thought she heard a loud noise, like something breaking, falling to the floor, but she couldn't begin to identify the sound.

Or even know if she'd actually heard it or just imagined it.

Everything was spinning out of control and she could swear she was leaving her body, separating from this heavy, heavy flesh that was anchoring her, holding her down.

The last thing she remembered before the darkness came was falling and hitting something hard.

Chapter 16

He'd called Emma the moment he'd gotten back into the car and started following the directions that Miller had given him. He gave her the same directions to the abandoned boathouse and knew she would be coming with backup. Given the circumstances and knowing how fast Emma operated, he was fairly certain that she was no more than five minutes behind him.

She might as well have been an hour behind him.

Tate couldn't shake the sense of urgency that was consuming him. Something in his gut told him that he didn't *have* five minutes. In this situation, even *one second* could mean the difference between life and death. *Hannah's* life or death.

So when Tate pulled up to the boathouse a few minutes later and saw Maddox's custom-made sedan parked some distance away, he bolted out of the car, barely stopping to pull up the hand brake.

The door was locked from the inside.

Abandoned buildings didn't have doors that were locked from the inside. If anything, there would have been a padlock on the outside.

Maddox was inside with Hannah—he'd bet his life on it.

Tate didn't bother to use his skeleton key tools to jimmy the lock. Instead, he put his shoulder to the door, slamming against it with all his might.

The door, weakened by weather and termites, splintered in its frame and cracked open.

The first thing Tate saw was Maddox with his hands around Hannah's throat. The next second, she was sinking, apparently lifelessly, to the floor.

Tate felt as if a broadsword had just slashed through his heart.

He was too late.

"No!" Tate cried, wildly enraged.

He didn't remember flying across the floor, didn't remember launching himself at Maddox, but he must have because he suddenly found himself pounding on the man.

The fury inside him flared out, coloring everything in hues of red. His fists made contact, over and over again, with Maddox's face and body. The skin on his knuckles tore and bled.

He kept on punching.

Tate heard a high-pitched buzz and realized a beat later that it was the sound of shrieking. It was coming from the sex ring mastermind beneath him. The man was begging him for mercy.

The irony of that was mind-boggling.

Damning Maddox's soul to hell, Tate promised, "I'll give you the same kind of mercy you doled out to those girls, to Hannah! How's it feel?" Every word was punctuated with another jarring punch.

He had Maddox's blood on his hands and he just kept swinging—until he heard it. A soft little plea, so soft that he *didn't* hear it at first.

It came again.

"No, Tate, don't."

Holding Maddox up with one hand, his doubled-up fist pulled back to deliver yet another reeling punch, Tate stopped. His heart hammering, he looked at Hannah. Her eyes were open, looking at him, and she was trying—in vain—to sit up.

Instantly, Tate released Maddox. The man fell to the floor, a crumpled, bloodied, sobbing heap, as Tate ran to Hannah's side.

Falling to his knees, Tate gathered her to him. "Hannah? Hannah?" Her eyes were closed again. Panic filled him as he begged, "Stay with me, Hannah. Please, stay with me. Oh, God, Hannah, I can't make it without you. You *have to* stay with me."

Hannah felt as limp as a rag doll and if she had indeed been awake a second before, she wasn't now. But he could detect just the faintest of pulses and he clung to that.

"It's going to be all right, Hannah, it's going to be all right," he promised her as he rocked her body against him. He held on to her tightly, as if the very action was the only thing tethering her to life.

Behind him, he could hear the pounding sound of approaching feet. Emma had arrived with the SWAT team.

"My God," Emma cried, looking at the unconscious,

bloodied heap that was Seth Maddox. She barely recognized the man. "What happened to him?"

Tate didn't even bother glancing in the man's direction. He was afraid he'd become enraged all over again and this time kill the bastard.

But that would have made him just as bad as Maddox. He had a feeling that Hannah felt the same way about it. That was why she'd rallied and called to him. To stop him from doing something he would eventually regret.

"He ran into a wall," he told his sister stonily.

Emma looked from her brother to the unconscious sex trafficker and nodded. "Works for me." And then she took her first real look at her brother—and the girl in his arms. Tate looked like hell. A very pale hell. "Oh, Tate, is she—?"

"Barely alive," he whispered numbly. "But there's a pulse and she's a fighter," he said, more to encourage himself than to give his sister an update.

Paramedics entered the old building, pushing a gurney before them. They were about to attend to Maddox, but Emma called them over to Tate and directed their attention to Hannah.

"Call a second bus to collect the trash," she instructed one of the agents who'd come in with her, nodding at Maddox. Turning toward the paramedics, she indicated the girl in her brother's arms. "She goes first."

Emma saw the absolutely haunted look on Tate's face. He looked as if he wasn't about to release Hannah to the EMTs.

As if he *couldn't*.

Placing her hand on Tate's shoulder, she did her best to try to comfort him. "Let them do their job, Tate," she coaxed gently. "They know best how to take care of her. How to save her life."

He made no move for a beat, no indication that he'd even heard her. And then a sigh shuddered out of him as he finally rose and backed away.

"I wasn't there for her," he said to Emma, watching every move the paramedics made. "If I'd been there—"

He couldn't blame himself. He wasn't at fault, Emma thought fiercely. "You couldn't have known and vermin like Maddox would have found another way to get to her." Emma gently tugged Tate out of the way as the paramedics slowly transferred the unconscious victim to the gurney, then snapped the wheels back into position. "You got him, Tate. You got Maddox. A lot of girls, as well as their families, are going to be grateful to you."

He nodded, barely hearing her. He was unable to take his eyes off Hannah. As they began to guide the gurney out, Tate suddenly came to. "I'm going with you," he told the two attendants.

There was no room in his voice for an argument.

Tate couldn't remember *ever* having lived through a longer night. The seconds had just dragged by, feeding into eternity without leaving a mark.

The moment Hannah was brought into the hospital, she'd immediately been rushed into surgery. A surgery that seemed to last forever. The reports, when a nurse *did* come out of the O.R. to deliver them, were not all that encouraging in the beginning.

For the first few hours, the situation was touch and go. Tate felt as if his emotions were attached to a yo-yo string, going up and down so much and so frequently, he felt dizzy.

The prognosis, when it was finally delivered after the surgery was over, was very guarded.

"But there is some room for optimism," the surgeon told Tate. A hint of a sympathetic smile faintly curved the man's thin lips as he said, "I suggest, Mr. Colton, that if you're a praying man, this just might be the right time to call in some favors from an authority higher than mine."

Praying made him uneasy. It meant the situation was entirely out of his hands. Tate didn't like losing control. It made him feel helpless.

"When can I see her?" Tate pressed.

"She'll be in recovery for another hour, then she'll be transferred to her room. I'll have a nurse come get you after she's settled in," the doctor promised.

"I'll be right here," Tate replied, leaning against the wall again. He felt more drained than he could ever remember being.

She wasn't doing him any good, hanging around here, Emma thought. But she could deflect some of the things he was responsible for doing.

"I'll go tell Villanueva you got Maddox," Emma said abruptly. Tate nodded, but she had a feeling that he really didn't hear her. She wished she could make him feel better, but she knew that only he could do that.

She gave his shoulder a squeeze. "She's going to be all right, Tate. Hannah's tougher than she looks. And when she comes to, tell her that we found her friend Mary Yoder and that she's all right. That should make her feel better," Emma told him with a smile.

"Yeah." His voice echoed in his head, hollow. Nothing was going to make any difference to him, wasn't going to matter to him, until he could see Hannah opening her eyes again.

* * *

Restless, Tate maintained a vigil by her bed. Though he knew he could do more good back in the field, tying up the myriad of loose ends taking Maddox down had created, he couldn't make himself go anywhere, do anything other than what he was doing.

Holding up a wall.

He belonged right here, waiting for some sign that Hannah was going to be rejoining the living.

"I'll spell you for a while," Emma offered the next day, popping her head into the room to see how both Tate and Hannah were faring. One was unconscious, the other might as well have been. She didn't know who her heart ached for more.

"Go, stretch your legs," she urged. "Get something to eat. Wash your face." She felt a sense of desperation as each suggestion seemed to fall on deaf ears.

Tate shook his head, rejecting her offer. "I'm fine," he told her stoically.

No, he wasn't, but she knew she couldn't argue with him about that. She'd only lose.

Emma tried another approach, one with a little humor laced through it. "I think the department has some kind of rule against wearing the same clothes for three days in a row." She nodded at the shirt and slacks he had on. She didn't have to ask if he'd changed his clothes, she *knew* he hadn't. "You don't want to smell gamy when she wakes up."

"*If* she wakes up," Tate corrected darkly.

"*When* she wakes up," Emma insisted firmly. "Tate, you have to have faith and believe."

He nodded, too tired to get into a discussion about it. All he knew was that he'd made his deal with God and Hannah still hadn't opened her eyes. How could a man go on believing after that?

Tate shifted in the plastic chair he'd pulled over to Hannah's bed eons ago. He'd lost track of how many days he'd been sitting there, watching Hannah. Keeping vigil. Emma brought him regular updates, as well as forcing him to eat the food she'd smuggled in. Sandwiches mostly, but she refused to leave until she saw him consume at least half of what she'd brought.

Tate tried to take solace in hearing that Maddox had been charged and jailed without any possibility of bail until his trial. The date wasn't set yet.

He knew that he should be happy to hear that the girls Maddox hadn't had murdered were all safely returned to their families and homes. For all intents and purposes, the case seemed to be all over except for the trial, which, a D.A. had assured Emma, was a slam dunk.

The upshot was that Maddox was going away for several lifetimes.

"It's over, Hannah. We got him. He's not going to hurt anyone ever again."

Holding Hannah's hand as he spoke, Tate felt as if his heart was breaking. It had been breaking over and over again these past few days and he wasn't sure just how much more he could take.

"Open your eyes, Hannah, please," he pleaded. "I miss your eyes and the way you looked at me. Like I mattered. Like you loved me."

Unable to hold back any longer, Tate laid his head on the sterile white hospital blanket and cried.

At first, when he felt the light pressure of a hand on

his head, he thought that Emma had returned and was trying to comfort him.

He didn't want comfort, he wanted Hannah to wake up. But if that couldn't happen, then he wanted to be left alone. Alone to share what would probably be the last moments he had with Hannah.

"You don't have to stay here with me," he said hoarsely, thinking he was talking to Emma.

"But I want to stay with you," the small, perplexed voice replied.

The second he heard her voice, Tate jerked his head up. He was afraid that his imagination had taken off again.

But when he looked, he saw Hannah looking back at him. Was he dreaming?

No, no, this was real.

He didn't know whether to laugh or cry. He did a little bit of both.

"Welcome back, stranger. You gave us quite a scare there." Almost giddy with relief, Tate pressed his lips against her hands, first one, then the other, kissing each in turn.

Hannah started to nod, but stopped and winced a little.

"My throat hurts." The moment she said that, she remembered. Fear entered her eyes as they moved about wildly—searching.

Tate instantly knew who she was looking for—and why there was fear in her eyes. "He's not here, Hannah. Maddox is in a prison cell. He's never going to hurt you again."

She seemed not to hear. In her weakened state, she only had enough strength for one thought at a time, one person at a time. And she needed to tell that person something.

"You found me," she said, her smile widening slowly. "I knew you'd find me."

His instincts had been right all along. If he'd waited for backup, he wouldn't be having this conversation with Hannah. She would have been dead.

He nodded in response to Hannah's simple words of gratitude.

"Sometimes things work out." He slipped his hand through hers and changed the subject. "The doctor said it was going to take a while, but you're going to be all right," he assured her. "Caleb's been by to see you every day. He's really been worried about your not waking up. He told Emma that he's going to stay in the city until he can take you home."

Home.

The word had been so comforting to her only a little while ago. It had been a goal she focused on to get her through her ordeal at the hotel. But now, what he'd just told her left her feeling very cold.

She looked at Tate, her heart in her throat. She'd lost years, she wasn't about to beat around the bush and lose another second of precious time.

"Do you want me to go home?" she asked in almost a hushed whisper, afraid that if she spoke any louder, her voice would crack.

"I want you to be happy," he told her. "And safe."

"You didn't answer my question," she insisted weakly. "Do you want me to go home?"

Had he not been so tired, so completely worn-out, he would have had the presence of mind to couch his words and proceed tactfully and slowly. And lie.

But he *was* tired and worn-out and in that state, he

said the first thing that came to him in response to her question.

"No. No," he repeated more strongly, discovering that the word felt right on his tongue even though he knew he should have focused on what was good for her. But he had to tell her what was in his heart. "I don't."

"Good," she whispered. "Because I don't want to go back. It's not home anymore, not like it used to be," she said, trying to find a way to explain what she was feeling.

Her eyes held his for a long moment as she searched for the right words. And then she finally just told him what was in her heart.

"You're my home now, Tate."

Nothing, he knew, would ever make him happier than what he'd just heard her say. But along with the happiness came a measure of guilt. Guilt because he knew that Hannah was very vulnerable right now and as much as he wanted her, as much as he'd discovered he loved her, he didn't want to take advantage of her like this. It wasn't fair or right.

"Hannah, I love you, but, honey, you are in no condition to make this kind of a life-altering decision right now."

He was wrong about that, she thought. Her condition, as he called it, had nothing to do with how she felt. She'd been grappling with this decision for a few days now—or at least the few days that had come before her last kidnapping. Tate had introduced her to a brand-new, wonderful world—two of them, actually. The one within his arms and the one that existed right outside those arms, out on the streets of the city.

"I won't be feeling differently tomorrow, or the day

after that. Or the day after that," she told him in a voice that was growing more firm by the moment.

He'd heard the trite line about eyes being the windows of the soul and in this case, he thought as he looked into hers, whoever had come up with that line was right. Because looking into her eyes told him that she believed what she was saying.

Still, he needed to hear it one last time. "You're sure about that?"

She nodded ever so slightly, her head still aching fiercely. "Just as sure as I am that I love you."

He didn't want her getting gratitude confused with love. He couldn't bear it if she realized the difference years later. "Because I rescued you—"

"Because your heart has spoken to mine," she corrected.

He couldn't bring himself to argue with her any longer. When she was better, and released from the hospital, enough time would have gone by for her to carefully think through her choice one last time. And when she came to the same conclusion and told him she was staying with him, *that* was when he intended to ask her to marry him.

And, he thought as he took her into his arms, she would say "yes."

He had a good feeling about this.

Epilogue

It was, truthfully, an oddly harmonious blending of people who were, for the most part, complete polar opposites: the peaceful Amish community was mingling with special agents from the Bureau and members of the Philadelphia P.D., as well as members of his family—extended and immediate.

It should have made for a bizarre sight.

And yet, somehow, it didn't.

In a strange way, it made perfect sense. They were all coming together to celebrate the recovery of the kidnapped girls—and to honor the memory of those who would never be back.

Tate glanced at the young woman next to him. He had a lot to be grateful for himself, a lot to celebrate. Having his family here just made it that much more significant.

Hannah's recovery—once she'd finally regained

consciousness—had been so quick, the attending phy-
sician at the hospital deemed it as close to a miracle as
he'd ever witnessed. He pronounced her well enough
to travel, which left the way clear for her to return to
Paradise Ridge—not because she'd changed her mind,
but because she was eager to see all her friends back
where they belonged—and trying to regain the peace
they had once known.

There was no way that Tate was going to let her go
alone. After what he'd gone through to find her—and
the hell he'd endured waiting for her to wake up again—
he was *not* about to let her out of his sight for more than
a couple of hours at a clip for the foreseeable future.

Hannah more than welcomed his company, eager
to show him where she had grown up. It was, after all,
the place that had made her the person she was now.
The place that had formed the survivor that she had
turned out to be.

They arrived just in time to take part in what turned
out to be a combination of new and old: an old-fashioned barn raising with the celebration of what was considered to be an outsider tradition: Christmas.

Tate looked around for the typical signs of the holiday season and found none. "Do the Amish actually
celebrate Christmas?" he asked Hannah, curious.

"Oh, yes, we do," Hannah assured him with enthusi-
asm. "I mean, we just don't have a Christmas tree or all
those shiny decorations that outsiders tend to put such
importance on, but we do honor the day."

His mouth curved. "About those 'shiny decorations
we outsiders tend to put such importance on,' I seem
to recall a certain young Amish woman being completely mesmerized by the giant Christmas tree she
saw in Rockefeller Center," he whispered against her

ear, reminding her of the occasion. The memory of her transfixed expression was one he was going to cherish for the rest of his life.

Rather than blush, as he expected her to, Hannah smiled broadly. "Who would not be mesmerized? It was such a beautiful thing to behold."

The area where they were, at a newlywed couple's farm, seemed to be filling up with more and more people. Taking Hannah's hand, he stepped to the side to get out of the way of several carpenters, bringing in the already crafted sides of what was to be everyone's project for the entire day.

"Do you exchange presents?" he asked her.

Hannah nodded. "Small ones. We give them to each other." She thought of the man she'd seen in the department store dressed as Santa Claus and the endless line of children waiting to sit on the man's wide lap and make their heart's desire known. "There is no jolly fat man to distribute them."

Tate nodded, doing his best to look serious. He failed. "Cutting out the middleman. Very economical of you," he teased.

Looking around the ever-growing gathering, he spotted Emma. With the case wrapped up, his sister was free to leave the Bureau, and she had. She was talking with Caleb. Her fiancé's three little girls were surrounding them.

Funny how his sister seemed to fit right into this life. If he hadn't known better, he would have said that she was born in this community.

There would be a wedding to attend soon, he thought.

Two, he amended silently—once Hannah set a date. He'd left picking a date up to her because he didn't want Hannah to feel that he was crowding her in any way.

Although she'd immediately said yes to him, he wanted her to be sure. Very sure. Sure that she not only wanted to marry him, but to be in his world as well.

Sure that she wanted to be with him.

But he wouldn't have been human if he didn't try to tip the scales a little in his favor. To that end, he'd bought a little insurance. He had it with him now and decided to give it to her before the "festivities" officially started.

Since that could be any second now, he put his hand into his jacket pocket and took out an envelope. He held it up before her.

She eyed it quizzically, then shifted that look to take him in as well. "What is this?"

"Only one way to find out," he told her with a smile, offering the envelope to her.

Taking it, she opened the envelope slowly. Hesitating because she didn't know exactly what to expect.

As she began to open it, he set her mind at ease a little by saying, "It's an early Christmas gift—although not that early," he amended, "given that Christmas is tomorrow."

A Christmas present. That meant it couldn't be anything bad, like a pretty card saying he had to go, or that he was taking back what he'd said to her in the hospital when she first woke up.

Tearing the paper away, she found herself looking down at a form that informed her she'd been enrolled in the Parsons School of Design for the purpose of obtaining a degree in fashion design.

It was like being in the middle of a double dream. Her dream prince was granting her fondest wish—to study professional fashion design.

Speechless for a moment, Hannah raised her eyes to his.

"Classes start the second week in January," he told her, suppressing his own excitement. "I thought you needed an outlet for all that designing talent of yours."

Thrilled, overwhelmed—no one had ever been this generous to her before—joy all but bursting out of her, Hannah threw her arms around his neck.

"I love you very, very much!" she cried.

He laughed. "If I knew it would get this kind of re-action, I would have enrolled you in that school a lot sooner." But he had to be completely honest with her. "I have to admit that I got the idea indirectly from Violet Chastain. I overheard her tell Mary Yoder that she'd pay for her schooling if Mary wanted to go to college. After everything that's happened," he said, referring to the actress's near-fatal stab wound when the woman had been left for dead while Maddox's men had kidnapped Mary, "Violet felt that Mary should have something good happening in her life as a result."

Hannah nodded, understanding. "Violet is a good person—just think, when her movie comes out, I'll be able to see it." The idea was incredibly exciting to her. She'd never seen a movie before. "And your sister Emma is equally as good." The immediate past forgotten, she was fairly beaming as she spoke. "Already Caleb is happier than I remember seeing him in a long, long time. His girls love Emma," she confided, pleased to be able to tell Tate something positive.

She was trying to make this easy for him, he thought. But there was no need. He was pleased Emma had found someone she loved so much.

"I know she'll be happy here," he told her, then added, "And you, I hope you'll be happy in my world.

I know I'm going to spend the rest of my life trying to make sure you are."

"No woman could ask for more," Hannah assured him with a smile.

Tate leaned in to kiss her, then stopped abruptly as he saw the sleek black limousine pulling up in the distance.

It looked suspiciously like the one that President Joseph Colton—a distant cousin of his late father's—traveled in.

But it couldn't be—

Could it?

"What is wrong?" Hannah asked, twisting around to see what had caught Tate's attention so completely.

"Is that—the president?"

Even as he asked, he had his answer as he watched a man dressed in a dark suit get out of the vehicle and open the rear passenger door. The president—wearing casual clothing—stepped out and looked around at the gathering.

A cluster of agents immediately surrounded him.

"At ease, boys," the president said with an easygoing laugh. "I'm among friends here."

Tate, with Hannah in tow, made his way toward the man he'd met perhaps a handful of times, predominantly before Joe had been elected to the highest office in the land. The Secret Service guard allowed him access—but kept watching him just in case.

"If you don't mind my asking, sir," Tate said to the president, "what are you doing here?"

"Well, I was just in the neighborhood," he replied, tongue in cheek, "and it occurred to me that I'd never been to an old-fashioned barn raising. Heard they were having one here. Didn't want to let the opportunity slip by." He rubbed his hands together as he looked around the gathering, then glanced down on the ground. The four sides were now placed at the ready, waiting to be pulled together and hammered into place to form the new barn. "Let's get to it, shall we?" the president suggested to the man who was his host.

Several of the Amish elders came now to extend their greetings and they took President Colton—as well as his Secret Service agents—under their wing.

As Tate, Hannah and his siblings all joined in, Tate looked over toward the leader of the free world and decided that this was going to be one for the history books—from start to glorious finish.

"I love happy endings," Hannah confided, whispering the words in his ear.

"But this isn't a happy ending," Tate corrected. When she looked at him, puzzled, he explained. "This is a happy beginning."

And it was.

He could tell he was right by the way Hannah smiled at him.

* * * * *

COMING NEXT MONTH FROM

HARLEQUIN® ROMANTIC SUSPENSE™

Available December 18, 2012

#1735 COWBOY WITH A CAUSE • *Cowboy Café*
by Carla Cassidy

When rancher Adam Benson rents a room from the wheelchair-bound Melanie Brooks, it doesn't take long for passion to flare and danger to move in.

#1736 A WIDOW'S GUILTY SECRET
Vengeance in Texas • by Marie Ferrarella

A lonely widow with a newborn falls for the detective investigating her husband's murder and discovers she has some very ruthless enemies....

#1737 DEADLY SIGHT • *Code X*
by Cindy Dees

Sent to the National Radio Quiet Zone to investigate... *something*...Grayson and Sammie Jo find themselves fighting for their lives—and falling in love—in the midst of a dangerous conspiracy.

#1738 GUARDING THE PRINCESS • *Sahara Kings*
by Loreth Anne White

Opposites clash when gruff ex-mercenary Brandt Stryker sets out to save a glamorous princess from bloodthirsty bandits in the African bush.

HRSCNM1212

REQUEST YOUR FREE BOOKS!

2 FREE NOVELS PLUS 2 FREE GIFTS!

◈ Harlequin®

ROMANTIC
SUSPENSE

Sparked by Danger, Fueled by Passion.

YES! Please send me 2 FREE Harlequin® Romantic Suspense novels and my 2 FREE gifts (gifts are worth about $10). After receiving them, if I don't wish to receive any more books, I can return the shipping statement marked "cancel." If I don't cancel, I will receive 4 brand-new novels every month and be billed just $4.49 per book in the U.S. or $5.24 per book in Canada. That's a saving of at least 14% off the cover price! It's quite a bargain! Shipping and handling is just 50¢ per book in the U.S. and 75¢ per book in Canada.* I understand that accepting the 2 free books and gifts places me under no obligation to buy anything. I can always return a shipment and cancel at any time. Even if I never buy another book, the two free books and gifts are mine to keep forever.

240/340 HDN FEFR

Name	(PLEASE PRINT)	
Address		Apt. #
City	State/Prov.	Zip/Postal Code

Signature (if under 18, a parent or guardian must sign)

Mail to the **Reader Service:**

IN U.S.A.: P.O. Box 1867, Buffalo, NY 14240-1867
IN CANADA: P.O. Box 609, Fort Erie, Ontario L2A 5X3

Not valid for current subscribers to Harlequin Romantic Suspense books.

**Want to try two free books from another line?
Call 1-800-873-8635 or visit www.ReaderService.com.**

* Terms and prices subject to change without notice. Prices do not include applicable taxes. Sales tax applicable in N.Y. Canadian residents will be charged applicable taxes. Offer not valid in Quebec. This offer is limited to one order per household. All orders subject to credit approval. Credit or debit balances in a customer's account(s) may be offset by any other outstanding balance owed by or to the customer. Please allow 4 to 6 weeks for delivery. Offer available while quantities last.

Your Privacy—The Reader Service is committed to protecting your privacy. Our Privacy Policy is available online at www.ReaderService.com or upon request from the Reader Service.

We make a portion of our mailing list available to reputable third parties that offer products we believe may interest you. If you prefer that we not exchange your name with third parties, or if you wish to clarify or modify your communication preferences, please visit us at www.ReaderService.com/consumerchoice or write to us at Reader Service Preference Service, P.O. Box 9062, Buffalo, NY 14269. Include your complete name and address.

SPECIAL EXCERPT FROM
HARLEQUIN® ROMANTIC SUSPENSE™

RS

Look for the latest title from best-loved veteran
series author Carla Cassidy

When rancher Adam Benson rents a room from the
wheechair-bound Melanie Brooks, he finds himself not only
a part of her healing process, but discovers he's the only man
who stands between her and a deranged killer....

Read on for an excerpt from

COWBOY WITH A CAUSE

Available January 2013 from Harlequin
Romantic Suspense

There was no way in hell he wanted the sheriff or any of the
deputies seeing Melanie in her sexy blue nightgown. He found
the white terry cloth robe just where she'd told him it would
be and carried it back into her bedroom with him. He helped
her into it and then wrapped his arms around her.

The idea that anyone would try to put their hands on her in
an effort to harm her shot rage through him.

"I didn't do this to myself," she whispered.

He leaned back and looked at her in surprise. "It never
crossed my mind that you did."

"Maybe somebody will think I'm just some poor crippled
woman looking for attention, that I tore the screen off the
window, left my wheelchair in the corner and then crawled
into the closet and waited for you to come home." A new sob
welled up and spilled from her lips.

"Melanie…stop," he protested.

She looked up at him with eyes that simmered with emotion. "Isn't that what you think? That I'm just a poor little cripple?"

"Never," he replied truthfully. "And you need to get that thought out of your head. We need to get you into the living room. The sheriff should be here anytime."

She swiped at the tears that had begun to fill her eyes once again. "Can you bring me my chair?"

He started for it and then halted in his tracks. "We need to leave it where it is. Maybe there are fingerprints on it that will let us know who was in here."

He walked back to where she sat on the bed and scooped her up in his arms. Once again, she wrapped her arms around his neck and leaned into him. For a moment he imagined that he could feel her heartbeat matching the rhythm of his own.

"It's going to be all right, Melanie," he promised. "I'm here and I'm going to make sure everything is all right." He just hoped it was a promise he could keep.

Will Melanie ride off into the sunset with her sexy new live-in cowboy? Or will a murderous lunatic, lurking just a breath away, add another victim to his tally? Find out what happens next in COWBOY WITH A CAUSE